PUFFIN

DRIVE

LESLEY HOWARTH

PUFFIN BOOKS

Published by the Penguin Group
Penguin Books Ltd, 80 Strand, London WC2R 0RL, England
Penguin Group (USA), Inc., 375 Hudson Street, New York, New York 10014, USA
Penguin Books Australia Ltd, 250 Camberwell Road, Camberwell, Victoria 3124, Australia
Penguin Books Canada Ltd, 10 Alcorn Avenue, Toronto, Ontario, Canada M4V 3B2
Penguin Books India (P) Ltd, 11 Community Centre, Panchsheel Park, New Delhi – 110 017, India
Penguin Group (NZ), cnr Airborne and Rosedale Roads, Albany, Auckland 1310, New Zealand
Penguin Books (South Africa) (Pty) Ltd, 24 Sturdee Avenue, Rosebank 2196, South Africa

Penguin Books Ltd, Registered Offices: 80 Strand, London WC2R 0RL, England

www.penguin.com

First published 2004
1

Copyright © Lesley Howarth, 2004

Set in Monotype Joanna
Typeset by Rowland Phototypesetting Ltd, Bury St Edmunds, Suffolk

Made and printed in England by Clays Ltd, St Ives plc

British Library Cataloguing in Publication Data
A CIP catalogue record for this book is available from the British Library

ISBN 0-141-31560-1

Contents

1. Crock of Gold

Break into the car with a screwdriver. Hack into the steering column. Bypass the ignition switch by hot-wiring a couple of wires. Gun the engine and drive!

Flooring it in a stolen motor, the headrush of speed as that smokin' road up to Brakenbury Hill opens out in front of you, your mates waiting at the aerodrome for that spec-tac-u-lar handbrake turn on to the runway. Haul on the brake till your tyres smoke and you're screaming around on rims. Chicken-race till you're running on empty and someone chucks a match in it.

And someone else gets out the petrol can.

Flames stream like water out of the seat you just left. Fingers in the ears for the giant Ka-boom! Then a ciderfest round the bonfire, drag up the busted settee with the worms of foam bursting out of it, watch 'em wilt in the heat before you wilt a bit yourself.

Then it's back on the last bus with the drunks.

Back to the vomit-smelling bus station and the railings stiff with rubbish, the tower block sticking up two fingers into the sky of the rest of your life. Remember the glow of the fire. The shared ciggies. The car seat glowing every now and then in the wind whipping across the runway. The smell of burning plastic. The taste of Tonic Wine, easy to score under age . . .

He told me how it felt, burning out to the old aerodrome in someone else's hot motor, your mates holding your legs as you stand up through the sunroof to give the finger to life, the tearing wind, everything else but the moment. Waking up next morning for another cold day in the city with nothing to do, wanting that feeling again. He told me all about it. The buzz. The thrill. The danger.

Then dangerous people had got to him. He'd been given a stolen car-key. Offered serious money to drive away a Mercedes from Portland Drive on the nod.

So far he'd said no, but they knew he went out to the Drome. It was obvious they'd use the joyriding to pressure him. He was messing with stuff that would change his life. I shook him. I tried to tell him. 'Wake up. This is serious stuff. You're not going along for a laugh when a mate of yours nicks a car. You're getting out of your depth. These people,' I said, 'they think you're something you're not.'

'It's called being at risk,' he said.

'Ben,' I said, 'you're my brother. I'll do anything I can to help.'

He just looked at me under that cowlick of hair. 'Simon wants me to stop too.'

'So stop.'

'I'm in too deep already,' he said. 'I'm not so sure that I can.'

— Confessions of Carmen Crocker

'Who are the Crockers anyway?' Luke demands in the chip shop.

Danny nudges him. Shut it.

'What, you can't even mention them now? How bad can they be?'

Luke moves up to the counter as a woman in a

distressed denim jacket turns away from it with sausages and chips twice. Her expression flickers over Luke and his brother Danny, coming to rest very briefly on someone standing behind them. The shop quietly empties as two or three people decide to get chips another time. An uncomfortable feeling grows and the reflection of a man with a head like a brick glowers at Luke and Danny from the mirror behind the counter, showing him just behind Luke's left shoulder.

'When you're ready,' Luke says, enjoying his own reflection between the jars of pickled eggs.

The assistant stops shovelling chips. 'What'll it be?' she says nervously, her eyes darting round Luke and Danny.

'Battered Crocker and chips twice,' Luke says. 'With Crocker sauce on the side.'

The assistant looks at him stonily. 'Cod or haddock?'

'Crocker kebab with –'

'Shut it, will you?' Danny gives Luke a dig.

'All right, I'm doing it. Medium cod and chips, four times.' Luke rounds on the man with the brick-red head. 'I'll pop you one if you poke me again – Sorry, I thought you were Danny.'

'Boyce Crocker's the name. You got a problem with that?' brick-head says, in Luke's face.

'No,' Luke says. 'Why would I?'

'We like to know who our friends are.' Reaching across Luke for the chicken curry with chips which the assistant hurriedly pops on to the counter, Boyce Crocker wipes his hands on Luke's beige hoodie. 'Got a problem with my family, have you?'

'If I knew who they were, I could tell you.'

'Luke.' Danny tugs him. 'Come back later, yeah?'

'I CAN FILL YOU IN IF YOU LIKE,' Boyce Crocker offers, the brick-red colour deepening around the back of his neck.

'Come on, Luke. Let's go.' Danny pulls Luke outside.

A bunch of hard-looking blokes in white hats watch them as they leave.

'You off your head or what?' Danny says, hustling Luke down the street. 'Those were his gang – the White Hats. Moving to Goss Side, Lesson One: Avoid Annoying Boyce Crocker.'

'How do I know who Boyce Crocker is?' Luke says. 'Look what he did to my clothes.'

'You know him now, all right? Let's come back later or something, when we're not going to get a punch in the face.'

Luke and Danny Couch, pronounced Cooch, turn left into Home Sweet Home Terrace. Home Sweet Home Terrace is a funny address, but Luke and Danny have got used to it already. Since their move from the country, a lot of things have changed. Before coming to the city, Luke Couch had been king of an outlying village where life was small-town and boring, cars got stolen somewhere else and no one had heard of the Crockers . . .

All he wants to do now is think about *Carrie*. Carrie lived in the shadow of the disused Goss Side gasholders, in a tiny alley off Gashouse Lane behind the cinema. She had smooth white skin and smooth black hair and she worked in the food hall at Fresnos. Luke and Carrie had met for the first time at the New Orleans Café, in the cinema complex under the gasholders. Danny had helped Luke ask her out.

The day after he, Luke, had met her, Danny told him straight, 'You want to look after her, you do.'

'Who?'

'That girl with the black hair I saw you with in that café.'

'I never saw *you*,' Luke said.

'Would you've noticed?' said Danny.

Their first date, Luke remembered not to fart. He remembered to ask her if she felt all right in those heels when they walked late at night to the bus stop. Three or four dates later, Carrie threw up on his trackie-bottoms after Luke fished her out of the Ladies at the end of a long night out. Come on now, he'd said. You're all right. And something had shifted between them because he'd looked after her, and because she, Carmen Raymond, had *let* him; and after that things were unspoken between them that didn't need to be said. He'd felt strangely honoured they were *his* trackie-bottoms. She half-lived over at his place. But still she didn't invite him over to hers. She curled up one night when he asked her, but he couldn't help mentioning it again . . .

'Anyway, I'm not hungry,' Luke says.

'Let's get curry and chips from the Chinese on Commercial Road.'

'Wish I hadn't met her after work.'

'Think Mum'll mind if it's not fish and chips?'

'Why does she always back off when anyone mentions her place?'

'Could get chicken chow mein,' Danny says. 'Are chips weird with chow mein? Could get prawn crackers and chips. Does sweet 'n' sour go with chips?'

'I don't want any chips. I feel sick. Are you deaf as well as blind?'

'What's with you?' says Danny, adjusting his glasses.

'Commercial Road stinks,' says Luke.

'I'm going there anyway,' says Danny, leading the way past the gasholders looming large opposite Home Sweet Home Terrace.

Across the road from their new house, the Victoria and Albert gasholders overlook Goss Side Entertainment Village. Under its stadium-sized car park the polluted soil which once burned beneath giant furnaces of the gasworks now borders Muscles Gym, Achilles Bar, a ten-screen cinema.

'You get tea and go home. I'll see you later.' Ducking through the wire fence, Luke sets a foot on the rotten iron ladder snaking up the side of a gasholder.

'Rowed with Carrie, did you?' Danny grins.

Luke stamps savagely up the ladder, shaking down rust and water over his back and head and into the hood of his hoodie.

'She dump you or what?' Danny calls.

'I just want to be on my own, all right? If that's all right with you.'

Danny swings off with the basket containing Mum's purse. 'Keep yours in the oven.'

'Don't bother.'

No matter how many times he climbs it, the view from the top of the gasholder always seems to soothe him. As Luke steps down gingerly on to the dome made up of rotten metal plates, fixed somehow to its frame instead of being puffed up with gas, a cool breeze from the harbour and the sea beyond lifts his hair from his face.

Danny crosses the street below, swinging his stupid basket. Everything's stupid today: the stupid cinema complex with its stupid action headliner; the stupid Victoria gasholder next door to this one, the Albert; the stupid Sun Fung Chinese on stupid Commercial Road; meeting Carrie Raymond after stupid work at stupid Make It All; Carrie's stupid locket that had dropped from her stupid rucksack and stared up at them both in the road . . .

He'd spotted it right away. She'd tried to pick it up. Tried to hide it from him.

'What's the C.C. for?' he'd said, dangling it in front of her, the initials spinning around.

She'd tried to catch it. She was lovely, with her creamy skin and smooth hair, the flame in her green eyes jumping up angrily. 'Luke, I mean it. Stop it.'

A heavy-set bloke had loomed large in the shadows under the gasholder. 'CARRIE. YOU COMING?' The colour drained out of Carrie's face as his voice rolled down the road.

'C.C. – Carmen Comehome,' Luke had joked. 'Carmen

Catch-me-if-you-can. Who's ape-man, by the way?'

'Give it to me, Luke.' She made a desperate grab for the locket.

'Thought you were Carmen Raymond.'

'It isn't mine, all right?'

'OY, YOU. COME HOME.'

'Come on,' says Luke. 'What does C.C. stand for?'

'Carmen Couch . . . It's a joke. Keep it. I've got to go.'

She'd turned and run away like a scalded rabbit. In case he'd see who was calling her . . . Where her home was . . . Who her family were . . . Maybe she was ashamed of him. Maybe she was just playing around and he, Luke, meant less to her than he'd thought he did. 'I really love her, Mum,' he'd said. He'd never felt anything like it, and now something wasn't quite right. He didn't even know her name. Carmen Couch. As if . . .

Luke hangs the gold locket on the ironwork surrounding the edge of the gasholder. Way below at the entrance to the car park, where the Village security geeks man a hut, a steady stream of cars turns into the Multiplex. Beside the car-park entrance a miniature Pizza King tees up for a busy Friday night. He and Carrie won't be sharing a King Cheese Crust Special there tonight, the cheese stringing between them, or sitting together in the cinema with their legs intertwined, not tonight, for some reason. ('Can't I see you later!' he'd shouted after her, but she hadn't even turned round.)

He didn't even know where she lived. Somewhere on Gashouse Lane. But she wouldn't tell anyone the number in case the White Hats hung around. That was what she said anyway.

Moving the locket and draping it in front of him on the curling metal plates of the gasholder, Luke watches giggling couples arrive as the cinema car park fills up . . .

'Yo, my man the gasholder!' Danny's unwelcome head appears at the top of the ladder some time later. 'You missed profiteroles. What's up?'

'Just thinking.' Luke shrugs.

'Give it up. What's with the locket?' says Danny.

'Leave it, will you?'

'Moo-dy,' says Danny. 'Carpark's filling up.'

'Nine o'clock showing,' says Luke. '*Deep Space Planet Nine.* Me and Carrie were going to see it.'

'Why don't you open it?'

'What?'

'The locket,' says Danny. 'It's hers, isn't it? Did she give it to you?'

'It doesn't open,' Luke says.

'Yeah, it does,' says Danny.

'Shut up or I'll —'

'See that?' Danny points. 'They're nicking it! See that bloke — he just smashed the quarter-light!'

Luke joins Danny at the edge of the gasholder.

'Black Golf!' Danny squeaks. 'Middle of the fourth row, right-hand side — see it?'

'You're right,' Luke breathes. 'Matey's hot-wiring it now.' He scans to the security hut. 'What do we do — shout?'

'Those deadheads?' Danny says. 'Probably in Pizza King.'

'Ring the cop-shop?'

'Be gone before they get here.'

'Can you read the reg?'

'No. Can you?'

In moments the car's in motion, zipping out of its parking space, lights coming to life, exiting on to the roundabout, caning it out to the Parkway.

'No way,' Luke says. 'That easy.'

Danny licks his lips. 'Going to open it, then?'

'Those Crockers, they're car thieves, right?' Luke says, as the Golf disappears into the night.

Danny's levering the locket against the side of the railings already.

'Think the blokes in the security hut are stupid or in on it?' Luke says.

'White Hats, aren't they?' Danny grunts. 'Of course they're in on it.'

'Give it to me,' Luke says, snatching the locket off Danny and breaking a nail in the side of it. 'Ow!'

Suddenly the locket springs open, and there they are – a family, with Carrie in the middle of them, smiling away like the photographer just said 'lesbian' or 'cheese' or whatever else they say when –

When a family comes to life. A man with a bald head, a faded-looking mother, and Carrie – younger, but recognizably Carrie – with, behind her, a brother a little darker, and behind him, Boyce Crocker, meat-neck and all. And inside the lid, an inscription: *Crockers Together, from Louis.*

'All right?' Danny says.

C.C. Not Carmen Couch. Not Carmen Raymond. Carmen Crocker, of *White Hats* fame. Carmen Car-thief Crocker, all the time.

'Fine,' Luke says. 'Why wouldn't I be?'

Carmen Crocker, of the family *everyone's* afraid of. Carmen Crocker, the two-faced liar.

Luke squeezes it together. The locket closes with a heartless little snap. It feels like closing his heart.

2. Vollie

'Stay away from the Drome boys,' I said. I begged him not to go joyriding.

He'd shrug and say, 'What does it matter?'

'You're clever,' I said. 'Go to college.'

'That's what Simon says.'

'Well?'

'I'm graduating in crime,' he'd say, with that funny curl to his lip. 'Anyway, it's good practice.'

'Practice for what?' I said.

'Come off it,' he said. 'You don't know Vollie works the margins?'

'What margins?' I said. 'What d'you mean?'

'You don't see for looking, sis,' he said. 'This family,' he said. 'No wonder it's patched together.'

The Patch Family, that would be us. Ben had nothing to hold on to, like me. I tried to keep things together at home. Ben had nothing to do. Nothing made sense in his life or knitted up with anything else to make a pattern. He did what he felt like. Hanging out at the Drome. Gambling. Diving off the citadel. Sweeping up at the casino. Simon was the only thread in his life. He did what he could, but it wasn't enough. Ben didn't care enough about himself to think what he was doing. So I started caring for him. I started keeping a journal. I started writing it down. It wasn't *really a journal. It was a way of seeing what I felt — what Ben felt — about it all.*

— Confessions of Carmen Crocker

Carrie had laughed at him. 'A DIY store?'

'Why not?' Luke said. 'What's wrong with Make It All?'

'Have you *heard* the music they play there?'

'Not selling music, am I? I'm marking prices on paint.'

Carrie had teased Luke about his summer job at Make It All in the pre-locket days, when they'd laughed and joked and she'd been Carmen Raymond.

Now getting up for work looks pretty cold to Luke. He's been there four weeks already and it seems like the rest of his life. It had been pretty easy to get it. The interview had been a joke.

'Summer holiday job?' Mason Greaves, assistant manager at Make It All, had handed Luke a form. 'Wear this red overall,' he'd said. 'Turn up next Monday morning.'

So Carrie and Make It All had come along one after the other. Luke plodded to work with Jasper Flashman from the betting shop round the corner, and hoped he wouldn't still be at Make It All when he was Flashman's age. And still the city air seemed strange and different from the country air he was used to, and the violet neon lights of the cinema complex over the road so temptingly close that Luke blew two weeks' wages on bowling, snooker and films before the novelty began to wear off.

Before he knew it, the unique smell of Make It All had begun to cling to his clothes.

'What's it like?' Carrie'd said.

'Like being forced to listen to sixties music in a DIY warehouse?' Luke said. 'It's hot and it stinks of plastic. Good thing I can nick rivets.'

'Rivets?' said Carrie. 'What for?'

'Don't worry,' Luke said. 'They're rejects.'

'Good, because rivet crime is taking off around here.' Carrie had seen and understood the wheeler-dealer side of Luke in a moment. Her brother, Ben, had more of the same, the only family member she talked about.

Shifting rivets at a tenner a hundred to Bargain Discounts down the road wasn't going to make Luke's fortune, but every bit of wedge earned out of work-time got back at Make It All for those unending plastic-smelling hours. And each day, crossing the road, the thought of *what he might do next with his life* began to fill Luke's head. Some nights he climbed the Albert gasholder and looked out over scabby Goss Side and dreamed of him and Carrie driving off into the sunset in some outrageously flashy new motor, and climbed down again and went home with rivet marks on his bum from the scores of metal rivets keeping the plates in place.

Pity he hadn't been in the market when the gasholders had been constructed. Someone had popped in the rivets red-hot. They'd expanded to fill the holes to make a gas-proof seal. There'd been a third, even bigger, 'gashouse' right where the cinema now stood. Gashouse Lane had been named after it. A giant retort house, where horizontal furnaces burned coke to produce gas night and day, had stood adjacent to it. Where Muscles Gym now opened its doors, a wash house for gas-workers had provided hooks for their grimy shirts and a place to wash to the waist. On the corner with Commercial Road had stood the Gasworks Social Club.

Luke spent some time in the library researching the area for a college interview. He fancied doing something with *people*. How about a GNVQ in Leisure and Tourism? Mum said. Mum said Research the area. Then you'll have something to talk about.

From the moment he'd seen them towering over the cinema complex, the gasholders had fascinated Luke. Now he knew something about them, they seemed to tower over his life and to see through everything he did. They towered over the locket incident. They tower over Make It All next morning, as if everything's just the same, though the world's turned upside down.

'She's one of them,' Luke says.

'One of what?' says Jasper Flashman, popping up behind the Special Offer One-Coat Exterior Paint advertised on a placard.

'A Crocker,' Luke says. 'How bad can they be? Would *you* go out with one?'

The thought of going out with *anyone* briefly crosses Flashman's mind like a train not stopping at this station. 'What did she say her name was?'

'What's it matter now? She could've told me the truth.'

'Stay away from Vollie,' says Flashman.

'I'm not afraid of the Crockers.'

'You will be,' Flashman says. 'Vollard Crocker's an evil little weasel with a chip on his shoulder and a bunch of apes for mates who do anything he tells them. Only one who's decent is Ben.'

'Ben,' Luke says. 'She talks about him.'

'Ben's all right,' says Flashman. 'He got some grief for stealing cars. Actually for not stealing cars.'

'How d'you mean?' says Luke.

Flashman shrugs. 'Story goes he smashed up a couple of motors they paid him to steal.'

'Who, the Crockers?'

'He got in with bad people. Then he didn't deliver. Went joyriding out to the Drome – the old aerodrome out on the moor road? They cane stolen motors up there, then torch them after they've thrashed 'em. Now he's hiding out. Mate of Ben's, Simon Bradshaw, he runs the casino on China Slip and he lets him kip on the floor –'

'How do the White Hats fit into it?'

'Are we gassing or stacking?' says manager Mason Greaves, on his way to the till.

'Gassing,' says Luke, stacking paint.

'Wear a white hat, you're with the Crockers. Don't wear one, you're against them. That's the way they see it. Flashman's jaw moves up and down in his anxious, spotty face. Something white in most people's windows because most businesses round here see it that way too.'

'How many Crockers are there?'

'Sisters, uncles, cousins – whole nest of 'em over on Gashouse Lane. Haven't you been to The Crock?'

'Ye-es,' Luke says. 'I forgot. Where is it exactly?'

'Standish Ope, off Gashouse Lane. It moves up and down the Ope – they own the whole row. Actually they own the *people* in the row. Wherever they are, people call it The Crock. No fixed abode,' says Flashman. 'That way you can't pin 'em down.'

She doesn't even have a home, Luke thinks. *Just a house that gets up and walks.* 'One of 'em ordered her in like a kid last week. I shouted, and he gave me the finger.'

Flashman nods. 'Shiny head like a snooker ball?'

'He was up the end of the road – maybe.'

'Vollie,' Flashman concludes. 'Story goes his hair fell out because it couldn't stand his face.'

'Could've been that meat-head who shouts all the time.'

'THAT WOULD BE BOYCE!' Flashman yells.

As Greavesie furiously draws his finger across his throat for the row in Paints to shut up before he shuts it up for them, Luke flashes on the bruiser in Goss Side Fry and knows that, in some twisted and not-quite-impossible world in which he and Carrie stayed together forever, he and Boyce Crocker might have been related.

That afternoon a shiny head like a snooker ball shows up at the Make It All helpdesk. 'Got mats for a Golf GTi?'

'You want the motor factors, mate,' Mason Greaves says pleasantly.

'Sell auto parts, don't you?'

'No.'

'Special Offer footpumps.' The man with the shiny head waves one in Mason Greaves's face.

'For pumping up airbeds,' says Greavesie, pressing the bell under the desk for Security.

'Car shampoo. Sponges. Manuals.'

'Extras,' says Greavesie. 'No car mats. I can offer you Lo-Price blow heaters or a nice line in late-flowering primulas.'

The man with the shiny head seizes Greavesie's tie. 'You taking the mick?'

'No. Are you?'

Luke cuts in with a paint chart. 'This New York Warehouse line – want them in with the kitchen paints?'

'Next to the bathroom anti-fungals,' says Greavesie gratefully.

Vollard Crocker drops him and wanders off. 'I insist on special attention, don't you?' he sneers, as people melt away from him in the aisles and the overhead mirrors in the bathrooms section show him pocketing plumbing fittings.

Security man Stuart turns up.

Greavesie nods down the aisle. 'Get Granville, will you?'

With Stuart and a hairy man named Granville who works in the warehouse behind him, Greavesie confronts Vollie at the end of the aisle.

'I'm going to have to ask you to leave now,' he tells Vollie from behind the shower-curtain display. 'I'm going to ask you to turn out your pockets. I should warn you that legal action –'

'Showing yourself up for what you really are,' Vollie sneers. 'Three to one, that's nice.'

Stuart tucks in his shirt over his beer belly. Granville looks darkly at the shower curtains as an advert booms over the loudspeaker: *Extend the life of your garden furniture with the Lorna Triple Plus range of exterior paints and creosotes, on offer this month with a free fold-up chair.*

'I'm going to have to ask you —' Greavesie begins again.

Trust Lorna protection for benches, summer houses, decking and picnic tables —

'Have it your way, then.' Slamming down a handful of brass gate valves, Vollie walks out, smacking over a patio umbrella as he goes.

'Been to the acne clinic lately, have we?' he spits at Flashman in the gardening section, helping himself to primulas on his way through the double doors.

Jasper Flashman flushes deep red. His acne is something that the mirrors of the bathroom display section constantly throw in his face.

Luke happens to be outside arranging patio chairs as Vollie leaves the store. 'Stolen many cars lately?'

Vollie whips round like a snake. 'What's that?'

'I said, Bought many chairs lately?' Luke goes in casually. His back looks casual through the double doors as they close casually behind him.

'Nice man,' Greavesie's saying inside.

'Some people are born evil,' agrees a customer at the checkout.

'He isn't all he's cracked up to be. I've seen him throw stones at people and kick their cars. Pathetic loser,' says Flashman, still burning from the crack about his complexion.

'Demonic little man,' says a pensioner with a stick. 'How much is the tiling grout?'

Luke watches Vollie cross the car park to a beat-up Ford Orion containing a very large dog.

Greavesie joins him at the window. 'He knows how to tap people's weak points. He doesn't care what he does.'

'Car mats for a Golf GTi,' says Luke. 'Saw one get stolen last night.'

'Didn't say anything, did you?'

'Who, me?' Luke raises his eyebrows. 'Want garden chairs priced next?'

When he meets Carrie after work Luke has two things on his mind. 'You lied to me.'

'Over?'

'That locket.' Luke watches and waits.

Carrie applies lip gloss. 'I know. But I had to go —'

'What kind of joke is Carmen Couch?' says Luke. 'Plus Vollard Crocker came into the shop. Thought you might know him.'

'Everyone knows him, don't they?' Carrie searches her bag for something which prevents her from having to look up. 'You haven't got it, have you?'

'What?'

She looks at Luke. 'That locket.'

He takes it out of his pocket. 'Want me to do it up for you?'

'I don't want to wear it, thanks.'

'Looks like it opens.'

'It doesn't.' Carrie drops it into her bag.

'So who's the C.C. on the front?'

'Carmen — Caroline, that's my name.'

'Carmen Caroline Raymond.'

'Quick, aren't you?'

'Why hide Caroline?'

'Why hide Patrick?' Carrie counters.

'You're joking, right?'

'All right. Patrick's grim.' Carrie giggles and kisses him. 'Luke Mark Patrick Couch, let's go back to yours, all right?'

On the way from Fresnos supermarket to Luke's house at Home Sweet Home Terrace, Carrie and Luke wander along the slippy walkways backing smelly Marrowbone Slip and the wharves around the aquarium. A poster slung over its new pine-clad extension with the wave-contour roof reads: 'Opening Here This Summer! The Deepest Tank in Europe!'

'Danny fainted in there.' Luke nods.

'You what?' Carrie makes a puzzled face.

'Mum goes, We're moving to Home Sweet Home Terrace. What? Danny goes. Cos you like the *name* or something? Because of Dad's job, she says. There's lots of stuff to do, she says. The aquarium, for starters. She wants to show us what a fun place Goss Side is. So Danny's leaning against this tank, "Fronded Guppies" and "Yellow Jacks", it says, then suddenly he's in the skate pond. The heat messed up his sugar balance. Too much sweating, Mum said.'

'How long has he had diabetes?'

'First he had bad eyesight. Then it kept getting worse. Now he injects himself. I call him Dan the User, but the olds go mad, so I stopped.'

'Good decision,' says Carrie, as they swing along the road together as though everything's just the same.

'Millions of car thieves round here,' Luke throws over his shoulder as they pound up the stairs to his room a little while later. 'The Village car park's a gift, security guys never see anything. You know you said Ben went joy-riding –'

'Ben isn't a car thief at least – he just gets with his mates sometimes.' Carrie selects a CD from the pile on Luke's bedroom floor. She slots one in, presses 'play'. 'Sometimes he gets carried away. He trusts other people too much. He isn't a bad person.'

A rap by City Life floods the room.

'What?' Carrie says.

Luke shrugs. 'You tell me.'

'He doesn't think. He does stupid things. Ben's actually really clever –'

'Where's your dad?' Luke says.

'I don't have a dad.'

'Everyone's –'

'My dad ran away when I was little, all right?' Tears stand in Carrie's eyes.

'Who made you go home the other day? Who was that at the end of the road?'

'I told you. That was my brother.'

'He pushed you.'

'He isn't perfect, all right?'

'Who was it, Boyce or Vollie?'

'You opened the locket, didn't you?'

'Why did you give it to me, then?'

'I panicked. I had to go. If one of us is in trouble we stick together, all right?'

'I heard Ben was hiding out.'

'So what if he is? I help at home and we try to get along, and even if I don't like everything they do, they're still my brothers, all right?' Carrie jumps up and stands angrily at the window.

'You could've told me,' Luke says.

'Yeah, and have you see me in a completely different way. I want to be who I am, not part of something people judge.'

The rap fades and another jumps up, this time about revenge, about checking up on people to see that they did what they said they'd do –

'I started up this carwash in the village where I used to live,' Luke says slowly, at last. 'Chat up all the old folk. Wash their cars. Rake it in. Money for old rope. People tell you their problems, you wash their motor, everyone wins. It was all right until the girl next door got pregnant.'

Carrie turns slightly. 'And?'

'It wasn't the same after that. Point is, I've got a big mouth.'

'Apology accepted.' Carrie sits down on the bed. 'What's it like in the country?'

'So boring you think your head'll fall off. Nothing to do, no transport. That's why I'm learning to drive.'

'Use City Buses. It's greener.'

'Only poor people use buses.'

'I can't believe you just said that.' Carrie gets up again. Between the curtains the lights of the Achilles Bar glare across from the Village car park. 'Can't learn till you're seventeen, anyway. It's not even your birthday yet.'

'I am seventeen,' Luke says.

'Thought you were sixteen.'

'I lied.'

'Why?'

'You know I'm up for college.'

'And?'

'I repeated a year at school. I thought you'd think I was thick.'

'As if.'

'Who's Louis?'

'Who?'

'*Crockers Together, from Louis.* Inside the locket, remember?'

'Always open personal things, do you?'

'Used to go out with him, did you?'

'Louis is my cousin.'

'Why d'you let your family push you around?'

'You don't know anything about us. Leave me alone,' Carrie says.

'Why weren't you straight with me?'

'Like *you're* always straight,' Carrie says.

Luke jumps up to block her escape. 'Why do we have to have secrets from each other?'

'We don't,' Carrie says. 'Goodbye.'

Luke flings himself over the banisters as Carrie clips downstairs and crosses the hall beneath him. 'C.C. stands for Carmen Crocker! You told me you were Carmen Raymond! You didn't have to lie to me. I wouldn't've lied to *you*!'

'*You DID lie to me, Mr Just Seventeen!*' the stairwell echoes back at him, as the front door closes on Carrie.

3. Cousin Wyndham

Ben came to me about the Mercedes. 'I panicked,' he said. 'I just took off. They paid me heaps to snatch it. Now I owe them a Merc.'

So they finally got to you, I thought. 'You owe who a Merc?' I said.

'Serious people,' he told me. 'They deal in stolen keys. They pay a monkey like me to go out and steal the car. They wouldn't leave me alone. "Lift this one for us," they said, "there's 200 quid in it for you. It's a one-off, all right? No pressure." They gave me the keys — and then —'

I looked at him. He was shaking. 'So you took their money,' I said. 'Then you didn't deliver the car. So give them the money back.'

'They won't see it like that. I'm hiding out with Simon,' Ben told me. 'They won't look for me at the casino,' he said. 'Simon works nights as floor manager. He doesn't mind me hanging around.'

'You can't hide forever,' I told him. 'Go somewhere before it's too late. You're clever, you've got options.'

'Options . . . yeah,' he said.

That was when I told him: 'Please, Ben, you've got to stop joyriding.'

'What's the point?' he said. 'I'd have to go backwards to put things right, and I can't do that now, can I?'

It was downhill all the way after Ben gave up on himself. Any car in an out-of-the-way place was an invitation to drive out to the aerodrome with his mates and burn someone else's rubber. The Drome boys melted away when things got serious. 'If they're your mates,' I said, 'where are they now, when you need them?'

'Maybe he didn't want to deliver the Merc,' Simon said. 'Maybe that was why he fouled up.'

Si never gave up trying to make Ben feel good about himself. 'Stop acting like you're doomed to failure,' he'd tell him. 'Start believing good things can happen.'

'They haven't till now, so why would they?' Ben said.

'Maybe you can't see them,' Si told him.

He didn't believe he could change. Ben took the guilt inside himself and swallowed it down with everything else, and it took him possibly deeper into himself than I'd seen him go before. The worst thing was what it did to him — what he did to himself.

'You're just making it worse,' Simon said. 'This isn't you. This is someone you're not.'

'Can't get any worse, can it?' Ben said. 'You don't know me,' Ben said. 'I don't even know myself.'

He wasn't a bad person. Simon knew Ben was clever. Simon could see he was stalling at a junction in his life. But Ben was living in fear. And fear does things to us all.

— Confessions of Carmen Crocker

'Cousin Wyndham's coming to stay,' Luke's mother's saying next morning as Luke rounds the kitchen door. 'Danny says he'll be nice to him, and I want you to make an effort. He isn't a very confident person. His mum says he's staying six weeks.'

'Six *weeks?*' Danny's eyes almost pop out. 'I thought you said six *days.*'

'Auntie Marion says he's been poorly,' Mum says. 'He won't be any trouble. It'll be nice to have company for you when Luke's out at work, won't it?'

'I don't need company, I need dosh,' Danny says. 'When did you find out?'

'Last night.'

'What kind of a not-very-confident person?' Luke asks suspiciously. 'The kind that needs looking after?'

'He doesn't like questions, he's shy,' Luke's mother says airily. 'Marion says he's looking for a job. Anything going at Make It All, Luke?'

'Can't you ask for me?' Danny says.

'They don't employ minors.'

'Their hats with torches on get in the way?'

'Ha, ha,' Luke says. 'He can have my job. Doesn't take much confidence to price aluminium ladders.'

'Greavesie tell you off again for yakking?' Danny says.

'This bloke assaulted him yesterday. Lifted him off his feet by his tie. They got it all on video.'

'And?'

'They're not pressing charges.'

'Why not?'

Luke shakes out the paper. 'Would *you* press charges against him?'

Vollard Crocker sneers out of an article headed '"Bull Terrier Safe," Says Owner.'

'These Crockers aren't as bad as they look.' Luke's mother shrugs on her coat.

'They are, Mum, they're petty crims.'

'Must've had a bad start in life.'

'Vollard Crocker's evil.'

'No such thing as evil,' Mum says. 'Just bad parenting. See how much holiday project you can do now, Danny. Luke's only over the road.'

'Yes, all right,' Danny mumbles.

'I'll see you after work, then. Remember what I told you about train times. Have a good day, Luke.'

'Bye.'

'So what are you really doing today?' Luke says, when the house settles after the door slams.

'Spending this.' Danny holds up a tenner.

'What's it for?'

'Meeting Cousin Wyndham at the station.'

Luke eats a Pop Tart thoughtfully. 'There's a map of town at the station, isn't there?'

'Plus taxis and a bus stop.'

'He's shy,' Luke says. 'Probably boost his confidence to get on a bus. What time is it?'

'Ten.'

'Three goes on air hockey before work?'

As Luke and Danny cross the junction to Goss Bowl to blow a tenner on air hockey and snooker, a faint niff of gas wafts across.

'These gasholders got bombed during the war,' says Luke. 'There used to be one where the cinema is. It split and this water and oil came out and caught fire and made a river of fire through the gasworks, and another one almost exploded.'

'Yeah?' Danny looks up at the dead-looking Victoria and Albert gasholders and tries to imagine what they are. 'They hold gas, right?'

'Yeah, and out on the harbour Lawrence of Arabia tested motor boats.'

'No kidding! Who?'

'This bloke who blew up trains in the First World War. He got famous and lived with desert Arabs and rode camels and all that stuff. Then he got too famous. They sent him here to cool off, and one day he saw a seaplane crash-land in the harbour and he jumped in a boat to save them, but he didn't get there fast enough and all the people drowned. So then he tested fast rescue boats. He had a speedboat named *Biscuit*.'

'How long did you *spend* in the library?' says Danny. 'Till your eyes fell out or something?'

'Least I can see,' Luke says. 'I don't faint in public places.'

'The aquarium made me feel ill,' Danny says, adjusting his glasses.

'Cousin Wyndham makes *me* feel ill,' says Luke. 'I'm not getting lumbered or anything.'

'I'm not either,' says Danny.

'I think you'll find you are.'

'You are, you mean. You're older.'

'You're Billy No-Friends at home all holiday.'

'You've got to share him.'

'You.'

And as they push each other across the car park, almost empty at this time in the morning, Luke and Danny sober down, and suddenly the image of a river of fire rushing between the gasholders and a red speedboat zigzagging to the rescue of a sinking seaplane out on the harbour makes the action pictures advertised over the cinema look pretty pale for once.

'He hid because of the newspapers,' says Danny, scanning a web-page later. 'Everyone knew he was Lawrence of Arabia. He called himself "Airman Shaw".'

'He chose to come *here*?' Luke says.

'They sent him here,' says Danny. 'To keep him out of the way.'

Danny clicks on a window and the picture of a wistful-looking man in Arab headdress flickers up beneath the heading 'Hero under an Assumed Name'.

'Lawrence of Arabia in Goss Side. Weird or what?' says Danny.

'Maybe he walked down Gashouse Lane.'

'Maybe he had a fag in it.'

'A snog.'

'A – never mind,' Luke says.

'Does it begin with –'

'Leave it.'

'Was he an evil person?' says Danny. 'Or was it bad parenting?'

'LEAVE-IT-I-SAID.'

In the act of saying, 'LEAVE WHAT?' Danny stiffens suddenly. 'Door. Get off. Mum's in.'

The footfalls on the stairs sound weary. 'Boys?'

'In here,' Luke calls. 'All right?'

His mother looks grey. 'Not really.'

'What?'

'Nothing,' she says, sitting down. 'Nothing that can't be fixed.' She runs her hands through her hair. 'But still, they could've – *done* something, I don't know.'

'What happened?' says Danny, his heart going out, sitting close to her, touching her.

'I had to take the bus home. I came out and the car was gone.'

Danny jumps up. '*Stolen?*'

'Borrowed. They left a nice note.'

Luke says, 'Did you report it?'

'That's where I've been all this time.'

'What did the cops say?' Luke says.

'They'll find it after they've solved all the murders. Put the kettle on, Danny. I've had enough for one day. Where's Cousin Wyndham?'

'Dunno,' Luke says. 'Maybe his train was delayed.'

'Danny? Didn't you meet Wyndham?'

'I was going to,' Danny says. 'But then I didn't.'

'We – thought he could meet himself,' Luke explains. 'Meet people on the bus.'

'We thought it'd be good for him,' adds Danny.

'Did you ring him?'

'No.'

Luke and Danny's mother passes a hand across her brow. 'Get me the phone. I told you the number of his mobile's on the pad – oh-seven-eight-seven-six-oh – meet people on the bus – nine-eight-two-oh . . . Wyndham? . . . Aunt Cath . . . Have you been waiting long? . . . Some sort of mix-up – sorry. We're coming to get you now."'

'What in?' Luke says simply, as his mother replaces the phone.

'Funny, isn't he?' says Danny.

'Shut it,' Luke warns. 'He's coming.'

The taxi ride from the station should've shown a pale and shaken Wyndham his place in the general scheme of things, Luke feels. Instead Wyndham jokes and snorts like a horse and seems super-confident about everything. Already he's annoyed them both by hogging the shower for ages and moving things round in his room and shoving things he doesn't want in theirs. They've escaped to Danny's room when Wyndham looks in and burps. 'Nice gaff. Fancy swapping?'

Danny's insulin kit lies open on his bed as he tests his sugar level. Wyndham watches with interest as Danny injects himself. 'Aunt Cath know you shoot up?'

'Does she know *you're* Jeremy Beadle?'

'Ha, ha, yourself and knobs on it.' Wyndham withdraws his head, oddly flat at the back, the hall light shining through his ears like lamps on either side.

'His head's flat,' Luke says.

'And the ears.'

'He can't help that.'

'But the rest.'

'Can't all be perfect, can we?' says Luke.

'What's wrong with you?'

'Nothing.'

'You've been a mood since last night.'

At dinner that night Wyndham eats all his sausages and leaves all his carrots and peas. 'I don't like vegetables,' he says. 'Can I have more mashed potato?'

'Potato's a vegetable,' says Danny.

'Pass the mash,' says his dad.

Conversation revolves around Mum's stolen Micra. In Mr Couch's opinion, car thieves ought to be shot. 'How's your mother?' he levels at Wyndham, out of the blue.

Wyndham colours up. 'Good,' he says. 'She's fine.'

'But how is she exactly?' says Luke, enjoying Wyndham's discomfort. 'When you say *good*, is she fit or just –'

'Choc-ice for pudding, Wyndham? Leave him alone, Luke, he's shy.' Luke's mother collects plates, skimming his warningly over Luke's head.

Wyndham swallows. 'I like Ben and Jerry's ice cream the best.'

'God forbid he should languish without it,' says Mr Couch. 'Any other preferences, Wyndham?'

'I'll get some tomorrow,' Luke's mother promises. 'Sure you've had enough mash?'

Luke clears his throat and gets up. 'Sorry, is that your foot?' he says to Wyndham.

All that evening Luke watches recorded *Futuramas* and moodily downloads music off the Internet in his room after trying three times to ring Carrie and getting phone-messaging. Wyndham and Danny play draughts and PlayStation irritably into the small hours on Danny's bedroom floor, determined to beat each other. Finally Wyndham crashes and goes off to bed with a single well-aimed kick at Danny's door.

Next morning Luke finds a note on the kitchen table. 'Please look after Wyndham,' it says. 'Make sure he has a nice day.'

'I *knew* it.'

'What?' Danny shouts through from the living room, muting Saturday morning telly.

'Looks like you're lumbered, big time,' Luke says, going through and handing Danny the note.

'WHAT DOES IT SAY AGAIN?' Danny bawls.

'"DON'T WAKE WYNDHAM TOO EARLY, HE MIGHT BE TIRED. FISH PIE IN FRIDGE. MONEY FOR CINEMA UNDER BISCUIT BARREL. LOVE MUM."'

'I'm not taking him to the cinema on my own,' Danny says. 'Can't you blow out Make It All?'

'Time and a half on Saturday.'

'Please, Luke.'

'No way.'

'Carrie could come too.'

'No,' Luke says, 'she couldn't.'

'Why? Is she doing something?'

'No,' Luke says. 'We finished, all right? Is that a good enough reason?'

A trumpeting noise at the door announces the presence of Wyndham in winceyette pyjamas. 'Better out than in. Can't you keep it down?'

Danny unmutes morning telly and racks up the volume to max. Wyndham retreats next door. Moments later the crashing of crockery announces he's found the cereal.

'*Did you see his PJs?*' Danny jumps as Wyndham's head sprouts from the hatch. 'What?'

'Spoons?' says Wyndham's face.

'Cupboard over the oven,' Luke says. 'Mind the axes don't fall out.'

'Dishwasher,' Danny says.

'Top banana,' says Wyndham's face, grinning and disappearing as he pulls himself back by the hair in a comedy ambush.

'Did he just say "top banana"?' Danny looks at Luke. 'Can't you get back with Carrie *just for one day?*'

'No,' says Luke, 'I can't.'

'I'll pay for popcorn and Coke,' Danny says. 'Hot dog – whatever you like.'

'What with?'

'Don't leave me alone with him, Luke –'

'What's on today?' Wyndham says, chomping over a bowl at the door with cheeks like ping-pong balls and Sugar Puffs studding his PJs.

'Danny's spending all day entertaining you and buying you whatever you want,' Luke says, getting up.

'Do they have pedaloes round here? I've never been to the beach.'

'You can dive by the pier and catch an ear infection. Be our guest,' Luke says.

'Nice red overalls,' says Wyndham. 'Give my regards to the bathroom fittings department.'

'Danny's all yours,' Luke says.

'Top banana,' says Wyndham.

'Thanks for nothing, Luke,' Danny shouts after him bitterly.

4. The Drome

'Look,' Danny says, on his fifth visit to the cinema with Wyndham, '"Cinema Ushers Wanted". Fancy it?'

'Fancy what?' says Wyndham.

'Job vacancy,' Danny says, so fed up with being shackled daily to Wyndham that he's willing to help him with his job search, which, apart from nagging Jonno the milkman, hasn't been going so well. 'Can we have a job application form?' Danny asks at the desk. 'Thanks. Fill it in here – on the stairs.'

Wyndham sits down reluctantly. 'Dunno,' he says. 'It says "Age".'

'Put sixteen,' says Danny.

'But –'

'Just put "sixteen",' Danny says.

Wyndham puts his tongue between his teeth and does a fair job of lying on the form.

In the darkness of his office, the manager hires him part-time. 'No nicking in to watch features on changeover when you're meant to be cleaning,' he warns.

'No watching features on changeover,' Wyndham

announces later at Home Sweet Home Terrace. 'Does that mean I can't watch the films?'

'Course you can,' says Danny. 'Major perk or what?'

'Congratulations,' says Luke. 'Keep your mouth shut, Wyndham. They can see your teeth in the dark.'

'What – do they show up or something?'

'Tombstones,' says Luke. 'Get fired for it. Distracts people from the screen.'

Wyndham snorts. 'What a load of rubbish. He talks a load of –'

'Rubbish,' says Danny. 'Yeah. Watch you don't get fired.'

Wyndham's job at the ten-screen Multiplex cinema involves standing at the top of two flights of stairs covered in popcorn and tearing tickets in two. In between 'features' he hoovers the aisles with a gang who call him 'Windy'. Sometimes he has to do ice creams down at the coffee bar, where long sausages named frankfurters revolve revoltingly on a grille. Wyndham soon acquires a taste for them, necking two El Presidente bumper-size hot dogs on every evening shift . . .

'Minimum wage,' Windy reports, 'but I get a big discount on film tickets.'

'Lucky to get it,' Dad reckons.

'Wasn't quite what Marion had in mind,' Luke's mother comments, as Wyndham goes out self-importantly.

'What did she have in mind?'

'She said he needs fresh air.'

'Got a ventilation system, haven't they?'

Wyndham and Luke come and go to their jobs, and

Danny — refreshingly — does nothing all day except mong around with his mates and stick Hubba-Bubba under the furniture, and over at the cinema coffee-shop the smoked sausages go round on their grille, and Windy's necked his twenty-fourth El Presidente when the Micra turns up on the moor road . . .

Danny and Luke hang by the phone as Mrs Couch takes the call.

'Thank you, Officer. Yes. L347 VGK. That's it. By the aerodrome . . . Oh, I see. And you don't know . . . No, of course. I'll be contacting them. No doubt they will. I realize that . . . All right. Thank you. Bye.'

'Torched it, did they?' says Luke.

'It's a write-off,' Mum says. 'Burned out on the moor road out by that aerodrome. I've got to ring Topaz Insurance — arrange a recovery vehicle.'

'Won't they do that?'

'I don't know,' Mum says. 'I've never had my car torched before.'

After lunch next Saturday the man from Topaz Insurance meets the Couches out on the moor road, at Moorland Motorparts, where the recovery vehicle has taken the Micra. The remains of Mum's car, which used to pick Luke and Danny up from school like a friend in need, stand sadly in a back lot, like a mate whose teeth have suddenly gone black or whose head has exploded.

'Wow,' says Luke. 'It's toast.'

'All the trips we had in it,' Luke's mother says sadly.

'Remember when Luke puked in the foot-well?' says

Danny. 'When we had to get up really early to go on the school exchange, and Luke'd eaten three cans of beans cos he thought he wouldn't like French food?'

Now the place of puking has disappeared, along with everything else, in the shiny film of melted black plastic which coats the inside of the wreck. In the remains of the car's charred 'face', one of its 'eyes' hangs out. Danny kicks the exploded headlight.

'It's a write-off, I'm afraid,' says the insurance assessor, bringing out a pen and preparing to fill in a form.

'You think?' says Luke.

His mother frowns. 'Shall we get on with the paper-work?'

After the olds have filled in forms in the plastic-smelling office of Moorland Motorparts and the man from Topaz has departed in a black Escort, Danny suggests they drive back via the place where the Micra died. Soon the approaches to the aerodrome unwind in dreary views of moorland criss-crossed with broken concrete.

'Over there!' Danny points to some crazy tracks leading to a black lozenge of grass. 'They came off the runway – that's where they ran out of petrol!'

Dad pulls over. 'So they set it on fire – marvellous. What a waste of space some people really are.'

A keen wind whips over the aerodrome, lashing the sides of Nissen huts forgotten and mouldering since the war.

'Stowe Moor,' says Dad. 'They evacuated people here from Tarmouth.'

'Same time the gasholders got bombed,' Luke adds.

'When did they get bombed?'

'They almost exploded,' Danny says. 'He's obsessed with gasholders.'

The car bumps over the old airstrips, rutted with grass and pitted with holes and cracks. Black windows flash in the sides of the distant control tower.

'Feels like they're watching us.'

'Who?' Mum says.

'I dunno.' Danny shivers.

Groups of ponies and sheep dot the stunted grass between the runways, grazing behind the broken buildings in the lee of the wind. Against a distant black line of trees, where the crippled control tower guards the lumps and bumps of old underground air-raid shelters, a factory sends out steam and a smell like old trainers.

'Cheese factory stinks,' Luke says.

'Best place for it,' says Dad.

'Leave it till the last minute, why don't you?' says Danny, as groups of sheep get up reluctantly and move off the warm tarmac of the only road across the moor.

Dad wheels round in a wide circle where a wire fence lined with rotten car wrecks guards a bleak-looking reservoir between the Drome and the road. 'Seen enough?'

'Let me drive,' says Luke.

'What, now?'

'Everyone comes here to practise. On weekends there's millions of learners.'

Danny and Mum change places and Dad moves into the passenger seat.

'Check you're in neutral, all right?' Dad says, when Luke's seat has been adjusted. 'Ignition. Clutch down. First gear. Handbrake off. And let the clutch bite slowly –'

Luke engages first gear and brings up his foot slowly and they jump away down the runway. He'll soon get the feel of the Focus. Luke actually drives quite well. Not for nothing have he and Danny thrashed Quad bikes round the field at the old place, and latterly a dilapidated Escort as well. Changing up through the gears confidently, Luke increases his speed . . .

'Steady on,' Dad warns.

'Shame about those old bangers littering up the place,' Luke's mother says.

'Got to practise driving somewhere,' Luke says.

'Practise driving?' Mum says. 'More like –'

'Luke, watch out!' Danny shouts.

Three or four sheep look up, unfazed by Luke's racing approach.

'Brakes and first gear!' Dad warns.

Luke's mind blanks the gears into a complicated H shape which he has to think through from the beginning before he can move his feet –

'Luke!' Danny squeals.

With five metres to spare, two of the sheep amble away as though remembering something. The two remaining sheep look directly at Luke through the windscreen in a boss-eyed stare that vaguely recalls the school caretaker —

Dad pulls on the handbrake. The sheep spin away as the Focus describes an impressive handbrake turn on the concrete and stalls in front of a settee.

Luke jerks back in his seat and stares at it, blinking. 'What happened?'

'You panicked,' Dad says. 'That's what.'

'Why is there a settee in the middle of the runway?'

'You expect a settee at an aerodrome,' Danny deadpans. 'Jumped out in front of you, did it?'

'Neutral,' says Dad. 'And change places.'

Previously blocked from view by a mouldy shed, the lumpy settee looks strangely vulnerable on the runway, like someone's old uncle they left out for the night and forgot. Around it other odd bits of furniture look equally out of place. It feels to Luke as though he's driven into someone's living room, appearing like some twisted dream in the middle of wild Stowe Moor for ponies and ewes to chat in.

'Someone lost their car seats,' Mum says. 'A settee, a lamp — they've even got a scrap of carpet. Wonder who put this stuff here.'

'The Drome boys hang out here,' says Danny. 'Higgin-bottom, Merchant — Pete Talbot.'

'How do you know them?' Dad says.

'They go up the snooker hall sometimes.'

'At Goss Bowl, you mean?'

'And Achilles,' says Danny, mentioning a bar before he can stop himself.

'You don't go to Achilles.'

'Luke does.'

It's a strangely homely arrangement – a settee and a couple of car seats round a table covered in bottles with an odd scrap of carpet in the middle. A gummy candle had dripped down the bottle they'd jammed it in. They'd even got a battered standard lamp with a traffic cone on top.

'All they want is a telly,' says Danny. 'They've got an old fridge over there.'

'Hang on a minute.' Luke's mother gets out of the car. She looks surreal in the living room on the airstrip with Stowe Moor and the cheese factory behind her, circling the little set-up on the carpet as though slowly realizing something.

They look forlorn and tattered, and now there's fag burns all over them, but the gash down the side of the front seat he made when he tried opening a carton of milk with a screwdriver still looks him in the face, and it suddenly dawns on Luke, getting out to join her, that *he'd know them anywhere*. 'Is that –'

'I think so,' his mother says, taking a seat in Drome HQ with the dirty fringing of the standard lamp just brushing the top of her head. 'They ripped them out before they burned it. These are *my* car seats,' she says.

For a week after that, Luke works miserably hard, burying thoughts of Carrie, glimpsing her occasionally on street corners, always looking away. Once he waves, but Carmen Crocker looks through him. Always a figure waits for her on the corner of Gashouse Lane. She no longer meets him after work, her slim legs flashing across the car park to join him outside Fresnos.

Finally Luke cracks. Instead of waiting outside it, he calls into Fresnos in-house café, The Servery, where Carrie's been working lately. 'Carrie here?'

'Who?' says the Servery assistant.

'Carrie – Carmen?'

'She left. Are you ordering?'

'Chicken Korma Special,' says Luke. 'When did she go?'

'I'm not personnel, am I? Rice or chips with that?'

Three nights later the Lucky Strike Casino on China Slip burns to the ground, and a few days after that Carrie rings Luke for the first time since the break.

'It's Ben,' she says. 'He's run off again. His friend Simon's gone missing in the fire. They think he might have –'

'Missing in the fire?'

'Presumed dead.' Her voice is hushed and strange. 'I knew something like this would happen. It's gangland down that street – and they were – after – Ben –'

'It's all right,' Luke says. 'He's OK, isn't he?'

'He's been hanging around the casino. They must've thought he worked there and then –'

'Calm down,' Luke says. 'Who?'

'People who don't like to be made fools of.'

'Have they found this Simon bloke yet?'

'I don't know.'

'Can I come round?'

'Luke, no. I'm sorry I called.'

'Carrie —'

'Sorry, I've got to go.'

For a couple of weeks after the fire, bouquets cover the steps outside the burned-out casino. Luke passes the site on his way to work as hoardings are going up and the lights saying *Lucky Strike Casino* fizzle and pop over the doorway, saying only *ino* before finally going out, perhaps forever.

An argument about the Crockers blows up at home.

'Ben Crocker wasn't *involved* with the casino,' Luke says. 'He hung out with his mate round there and someone saw him running away.'

'The Crockers are always involved,' Dad says.

'You don't *know* that,' Mum says. 'It was probably gang rivalry or something.'

'Exactly,' Dad says. 'The Crockers.'

'They say Ben Crocker's the best of the bunch. Whatever happened to giving him the benefit of the doubt?' Mum says.

Luke glowers at her, clinching it by finding a piece in the paper which says that foul play is suspected. A fight had occurred at a rival casino. The Lucky Strike bouncers had smashed someone in the head in revenge. Now the Lucky Strike had burned down. 'Casino Wars', the article was headed. 'He thinks it's his fault,' Luke finishes.

'Who?' Dad says.

'Ben,' Luke says, unable to finish the sentence without dobbing Ben in properly and ruining his own argument. *Ben Crocker was hiding out after they paid him to steal a top-of-the-range*

Merc. He thinks they torched the casino to get at him. 'So they say. Anyway, I don't even know him.'

'Carrie's got a brother called Ben, hasn't she?' Mum asks innocently.

'What if she has?' says Luke, breaking into a sweat.

'We haven't seen her lately. Everything all right?'

'Why wouldn't it be?' Luke says.

Visions of Ben Crocker, Carrie's dark-haired brother in the locket photograph, swim in Luke's mind all day. What's he like now? Hard, mad, misunderstood – the victim of a nightmare family? Had he – had Carrie – wanted to tell him something? *Had throwing him, Luke, the locket been a cry for help?*

The whole world doesn't revolve around the Crockers, Luke reminds himself. Instead, it revolves around Wyndham. Security at the Multiplex has been tightened since the fire and no gang colours are allowed.

'I only asked him to post it in the box!' Wyndham wails in the living-room doorway a couple of days later, after bursting in and slamming the front door. 'It's a perspex box. You can see them. We give them back after the film.'

Danny and Luke look up over the telly. 'Come in, you nerd. Post what in the box?'

A rash of white hats has been dotting the streets as the war between local casinos hots up. The Multiplex has hired new security guards. Oddly, Boyce Crocker's one of them. The clubs on either side of Goss Bowl have beefed up security too. And over all the troubled side of town the gasholders drip and throw shadows . . .

'His huh – *hat*,' Wyndham chokes, bursting into a great gust of sobbing. 'He shoved me – in the –'

'Back? Guts? Nuts?'

'*Face*,' Wyndham says, rubbing his sleeve across it.

'Who did?' Danny says.

'Bloke with a – shiny –'

'Car? Ring? Nose?'

'– *head*.'

'Thin or fat?' Luke says.

'Thuh – thuh –'

'Vollard Crocker,' Luke says.

'Hullo, what's up with young Wyndham?' Dad says, breezing in.

'Hat-posting tragedy,' Luke says.

'Wrong hat or wrong post box?'

'Wrong punter,' Luke says, torn between hating Wyndham and hating Vollard Crocker, surprising himself by preferring Wyndham hands down. 'Someone pushed him for confiscating their hat.'

'Tell the manager, did you?'

Wyndham shakes his head.

Dad takes Wyndham's hand in his bear-like grasp. 'Come on. Let's get some chips.'

Wyndham sniffs. 'All right.'

Luke watches them walk down the street together, Dad's head stooping to tell Wyndham something funny about his day to take his mind off the hat tragedy and make Wyndham feel better. And as they swing down the street together and the sunlight lances between them on the crossing, making Wyndham look very young and Dad even more bear-like, and they look like they're sharing a secret or just having a laugh without him, Luke even feels left out . . . What must it be like to have no dad?

Luke's rage crystallizes that night. If that's what he thinks he can do in the cinema, *what must Vollard Crocker be like at home?* Suddenly the abyss over which Carrie must live every day of her life opens under Luke's feet. This is the man who lifted Mason Greaves off his feet by his tie. If Vollie pushes cinema staff around, what wouldn't he do over the breakfast table? Could the vague-faced mum in the locket stop Vollie from – from what? Come to think of it, Carrie never mentions her mother.

Maybe Carrie got into trouble when she gave him, Luke, her locket. *Crockers Together, from Louis.* Maybe they all had lockets. Lost our locket, have we? Vollie's sneering voice echoes through Luke's nightmares. WELL? Boyce Crocker intrudes. WHERE IS IT, THEN? Again and again a figure silhouetted against the gasholders orders Carrie home. Carrie's face streams with tears. It's Ben, she says. You don't understand –

Luke sits up in bed.

Normal people don't rush home, change their name, have a home that moves up and down the street, or live in fear of their brothers. Carrie needs help – *his* help. Pulling on his clothes, Luke slips downstairs under the moon. As he closes the front door, only the insistent dripping of the kitchen tap and Wyndham gibbering in his sleep in his bedroom upstairs disturbs the silence of the house and masks the click of the door.

Luke slips across the junction and under the shadow of the gasholders, the moonlight picking out every rivet and plate in their sides, every flake of rust on every gantry, his feet slapping the pavements, silent for once, as in the cold light of the week-night small hours even the Entertainment Village sleeps. A right turn down Gashouse Lane, left on to Standish Ope –

The sound of breaking glass! Luke listens briefly. Someone cracking a quarter-light in some unguarded motor. Lonely area to leave a vehicle. Asking for it really.

The cobbles shine on Standish Ope outside what could be Carrie's house. The 'Opes', short for openings in the rows of terraces, are usually cobbled rat-runs left over from bleaker times when the wharves were home to mariners and stevedores, also with movable homes, who didn't care where they stayed. The house fronts, which could all be Carrie's, look down on Luke like cards in a poker hand. She never let him see her turn into Standish Ope. Still, one of them had a feeling about it. Outside a house near the end of the street a gnome with a gash in its side watches over a pile of milk bottles. He'd walked this way a million times, wondering if this was the one. 'The Crock', Carrie's movable home, impossible to nail down – could this be it at the moment? Luke looks up at its blank windows. If Carrie were sleeping behind its walls, surely there'd be a sign, something of hers in the window, a difference in the feel of the place?

The stars peer down over her gutter, as if to say, *This is the house. Here she is, only metres away, sleeping softly, so near, and so far.* Luke wills her to appear at the window, but the moon shines coldly down and the cobbles gleam and a dog yowls somewhere over Marrowbone Slip and a chilly wind lifts down the street. Luke tries to penetrate its bricks – *I'm here, I'm outside, look out!* But instead of Carmen Crocker, a really quite ordinary house in a greasy street looks down.

He could have rattled its door.

He could have howled at the moon.

He could have shouted up and down, *Wake up, this is important! I'll always look after you, like the time you threw up on my trackies!*

Instead Luke turns up his collar and walks back via Marrowbone Slip. A few chips float on the oily water slapping the wharves. A plaque in a wall informs him that 'Here bones imported from France were shipped upriver to bone-crushing mills to enrich local fields with fertilizer.'

Little bits of bones over the fields . . . A picture of the village he's left jumps up in Luke's mind: the crossroads outside his old house in the moonlight, foxes barking and cows bawling in the distance, owls flitting white as ghosts, bats flickering, badgers flopping down hedges following their secret paths, while underground moles work all night . . .

A thousand images of the fields round his old home rush like leaves through Luke's mind, trailing an idea behind them. A mole working underground – why not?

If he couldn't help her from outside, *he'd help Carrie from* within. His own family had never met Cousin Wyndham, after all. He himself wasn't known to the Crockers, Carrie had seen to that. How about posing as a distant member of the family to get an 'in' at The Crock, working undercover to see her, find out what was going on? What should he call himself? Cousin Wayne? Cousin Darren?

Luke climbs the Victoria gasholder on his way home to show himself that he came out for something other than hanging around outside Carrie's house. The Vicky's quite a bit bigger than the Albert and the view's pretty positive from the top. A sleeping city, not good, not bad. Helping Carrie's a plan, isn't it? A plan gives you a future, doesn't it, one way or the other?

Beyond the tinkling masts in the harbour the red and green lights of oddly named buoys swing in the darkened Sound – Malaboys, China, Kildare and New Grounds, marked on the shipping maps Luke had seen framed in the library. Behind its citadel the city lies glowing like a jewel, the turquoise wave of the aquarium roof surfing the lights of clubland and the city-centre neon beyond. *Imagine a river of fire, bombs over the Palisades Shopping Mall, people out on Stowe Moor watching the city burn.* Weird to think about it now, while the city glitters quietly below and only the odd siren echoes the thought of all that. How hard would it have been during the war to imagine a scene like this? How hard was it now to imagine life then? At his college interview for the GNVQ course in Leisure and Tourism, for which he'd swotted stuff up in the library, Luke had tried to explain.

'They were blacked out during the war, they never had

any lights, so nothing looked the same, Goss Side was this huge great gasworks, the men wore these iron-soled clogs to work cos the floors by the furnaces were hot, they never washed their backs cos they thought it would hurt their kidneys, they'd never've been able to imagine stuff like Goss Bowl or the cinema –'

The admissions tutor had cleared his throat politely. 'The fact is, Luke, we get a lot of young people coming for interview who don't know what they want to do.'

The pink lights of Muscles Gym dance on the neighbouring gasholder, now like a castle or a galleon, a theme-park addition to the Entertainment Village, no different from the giant pizza lighting up Pizza King. But a drama had once been enacted up here which Luke had been unable to get out of his mind.

'I know that,' he'd said. 'But I do.'

The admissions tutor had looked at Luke. 'So how would you promote tourism in your area?'

Luke had been ready for this. This was the point of the library. 'There's seaplanes and rescue boats. Lawrence of Arabia. And the gasworks.'

'And how would the gasworks feature?' The tutor had raised his eyebrows.

'It's the night of 14 April 1940,' Luke had begun, his face lighting up expressively and his arms and hands conjuring events, 'and there's incendiary bombs being dropped and fires all over the city. Incendiaries are, like, fire bombs. So one of them falls on the Vicky – the Victoria gasholder on Goss Side, built 1881. If it blows up filled with gas, there'll be this *giant* explosion and hundreds of people'll be killed. I've forgotten how many cubic litres of gas, but –'

'I can imagine. So?'

'So three men climb up the gasholder to fight the fire, even though it could blow at any minute . . . Can you *imagine* climbing this tower of gas with a fire burning on top of it?'

The admissions tutor mopped his brow. 'I'm assuming this went well.'

'Their names were Ned Beale, Robert Turner and Eden Fishlake, they had iron clogs on which burned their feet, they put out the fire with these canvas hoses and stopped the gas exploding, then the boss of the gas company gets an MBE for saving the gasworks, and they get bronze medals, which I don't think's fair –'

The admissions tutor watched Luke's face.

'– when it was old Ned and Bob and Eden who went and burned their feet saving the area, including Home Sweet Home Terrace –'

'That's where you live?'

Luke had nodded.

'It's on a major bus route. Numbers 43 and 54 should bring you to college.'

The admissions tutor had stood up and smiled, and Luke had taken his hand, and with it a passport to college and a place on the course he wanted, without even going through his lack of decent grades at GCSE, and all *because of this gasholder* . . .

Luke recrosses the dome to the ladder. *Kuh-bum, kuh-boom.*

Big as a church, the space underneath sends back a sound like doom. A light winks on in the security booth at the entrance to the car park. Boyce Crocker'll be out in a minute, throwing his weight around.

Luke climbs thoughtfully down the steps which Ned and Bob climbed up that night. It was the Vicky that had almost exploded. These same dripping walkways had had canvas hoses hauled over them, had witnessed the drama that night as Eden and Ned had stamped around on the hot metal dome in their gasworker's iron-soled clogs with the courage to fight for what was theirs, courage missing tonight as, over neon-lit Goss Side, everyone huddles indoors.

The Gashouse Lane Volunteers had saved the area for the White Hats to lord it over and destroy in a different way. If he can find out what makes them tick, maybe he, Luke, can be the Ned or Bob of The Crock, get to see Carrie, and maybe free Goss Side from fear and corruption . . . Why not?

Big ideas are all right, but Carrie'll have to know, so's she won't spill, or betray him by a sudden exclamation. Will she get that it's all for her, the mole in the middle of a wolf pack, like the undercover cop who makes a wrong move and gets taken for a ride in the country between a couple of guys in big coats whose idea of a joke is to get him to dig his own grave? The sort of idea no one who wasn't mad or gutted would try?

A brave idea.

If he can hack it.

5. Driving Lessons

Ben went wild after he lost Simon in the fire. He ran off, came back, ran off.

'It's all my fault,' he'd rage. 'Si was working that night, I know he was.'

'They haven't found anyone yet,' I said.

'Why are there flowers on the steps of the casino, then? Where is he, then?' he'd want to know.

Ben and Si, they were close. They'd been through a lot together. Everyone in my family's been through hell and back since Mum died. Two good things came out of the fire. Ben came home for a while. And it brought me and Luke back together.

Vollie'd talked it out with Ben the night before. 'You stay here, all right? We're a family, aren't we? Stop running around and blabbing stuff all over town. Simon get crisped, did he? Looks like he had it coming.'

I heard the crash. Ben had put his fist through a pile of plates. Boyce was bandaging his hand when I opened the kitchen door. 'What?' Vollie said. Ben slammed out. There was blood all over the floor.

I ran upstairs and rang Luke. He was the only thing I had left to hold on to.

— Confessions of Carmen Crocker

'Why can't I be one of them?' Luke points to two obscure cousins on the genealogical web-page headed 'Crocker' thrown up by Danny's search.

'Hilary and Philippa, you mean? I'm assuming you bought a wig.'

'Duncan Kirkpatrick Crocker, then,' says Luke, looking more closely.

Danny clicks on Duncan. 'Born 1962. Emigrated to Australia.'

'There must be some distant cousin about my age.'

'Milton Crocker, born '96 . . . Too late. Arnold, Ronald and Donald, all dead . . . Kylie, Danni and Jason Crocker –'

'Go to "Couch" for a laugh,' Luke says.

Danny enters 'Couch' under 'surname' in the list titled 'Trace Your Family Tree'.

'Go to Wyndham,' Luke says.

Danny enters 'Wyndham Couch'.

'No Results,' says the search.

'Marion's mum's cousin, isn't she?' says Luke. 'What's their surname?'

'Dunno.'

'You helped him fill out a job form.'

'Nettlebum or something,' says Danny.

'She should still be on a branch of the tree.' Luke pages across. 'Here – Marion Jane Brownlow marries Clifford Nettlefold. Sons Harris and Wyndham Nettlefold, born '83 and '85.'

'That can't be right,' says Danny. 'That makes him eighteen. He looks about twelve or something.'

'Must've entered the dates wrong,' Luke says. 'That or he isn't –'

'Luke!' Mr Couch calls upstairs. 'Diana Buchanan's here!'

'Diana who?' Luke bawls.

'Buchanan!' his father shouts up. 'She's asking for you. Front door.'

Luke hammers downstairs to find a woman in a navy trouser suit with a clipboard under her arm. 'Luke Couch? Diana Buchanan.'

'Cooch like pooch, not like a settee,' Luke says coldly.

'And this'll be your first lesson?'

FIRST GEAR DRIVING SCHOOL announces the electric-blue 206 behind Diana Buchanan. *High First-time Pass Rates. Nervous & Mature Pupils a Speciality. Friendly and Patient. First Lesson Free. Block-booking Discount.*

'Driving lessons, right,' Luke says, remembering the call he made as the situation dawns on him at last. 'Sorry, but when I rang up, I thought it might be –'

'A man?'

'A Fiesta,' Luke sweats, 'or a Ka.'

'Most learners get on well with the 206.' Diana Buchanan eyes Luke over her clipboard. 'First lesson's free, subsequent lessons are fifteen pounds for thirty minutes, twenty-seven the hour, unless you go for block-booking, in which case savings can mount up over a course of twenty lessons. Provisional licence?'

Luke darts in and fetches it off the sideboard. 'Be good to drive to college,' he says conversationally. 'I just got a place and I'm –'

'Sign here.' Diana Buchanan hands Luke her clipboard. 'Let's make a start. This side.'

'What, now?'

'That is,' says Diana Buchanan, 'if you want to learn to drive.'

After a seat-belt fitting and a stiff lecture on starting up and pulling away and a million gurning glances into his mirror, Luke indicates and pulls out. Of course he wants to learn to drive. All his life in the country he'd longed to be able to go somewhere *when he wanted to*. No nagging the olds for a lift or hanging around for buses to Tarmouth which came through the village *once a week* and then were cancelled completely.

It was all right if you could get to the local town, three miles away, to pick up bus connections. If you couldn't, you were stuffed. How cool would it be to just jump in your motor and drive! Wherever – whenever – you wanted! No killing yourself uphill on your bike for a bag of Haribo Mix at the newsagent's. No begging and pleading for a scooter, no rows over taxis to town or lifts back late at night from mates' houses in neighbouring villages, no more nagging about having a car when he was older and *driving wherever he wanted to and never having to ask* . . . This is it, driving lessons at last!

It was hard to live in the country if you were young and had a mind of your own, or a life. Frustration had started early. Once, when he was eight, Luke had fallen out with his mother. He'd wanted to go into town after school – obviously – to get the *Simpsons* stickers he'd been saving up for. For some reason, after a busy day at work, his mother hadn't understood how important it was to get them *straight away*.

'I'm not going into town now,' she'd said. 'We'll get them on Saturday.'

It had ended with Luke screaming, 'I'm GOING *to town and I'm GETTING THEM and YOU can't stop me anyway!*' and running across the road.

He'd turned up on Mrs Oliff's doorstep. 'Luke,' she'd said, 'is something the matter?'

Eight-year-old Luke had set his chin. 'Are you going to town? Cos I need to get some stickers.'

Mrs Oliff had registered the red eyes and blubbery face and had understood immediately that this was a life-changing moment. 'As it happens,' she said, 'I've got a few things to pick up. Come on, we'll go and get them.'

Luke had run home to tell Mum, and he and Mrs Oliff had gone to town together. On the way home with his stickers – not the ones he'd wanted, but ones *almost* as good – Luke had regaled Mrs Oliff with the plotlines of three films and vital information about his favourite metal band, Headcrush. Mrs Oliff had wanted to know the name of Headcrush's lead singer. She'd wanted to know the name of their latest CD. She'd wanted to know in which order he, Luke, was going to stick his stickers into his sticker book.

Luke had never forgotten the empowering lift to town of that day. His mother had respected him for it. When she and Mrs Oliff had chatted over the wall, they'd agreed on

Luke's outstanding resourcefulness, *and here he is, officially driving at last* —

'Stop!' shouts Diana Buchanan, standing on the dual controls as the Peugeot drifts across three lanes of traffic and stalls on the Riverpark roundabout. 'Give way to the right! I asked you to stop at the junction!'

'Sorry. I wasn't thinking,' says Luke, his mind still on *Simpsons* stickers.

Diana Buchanan knocks the gear stick into neutral and waves other drivers by. 'Let's be clear about this. When I rap the dash with my biro, I mean *emergency stop.*'

'I thought you were throwing a wobbly with your pen,' Luke apologizes.

'I can see we've got a challenge ahead of us. Pull away whenever you're ready,' says Diana Buchanan.

Three streets away, Carmen Crocker turns the key in a Golf GTi while it's still in gear. The car leaps forward and stalls.

'Kangaroo petrol,' says Carrie.

'NEUTRAL!' bawls Boyce Crocker, the veins standing out on his head. 'HANDBRAKE! IGNITION! CLUTCH! FIRST!'

'I'm not sure your teaching me to drive is a good idea,' says Carrie.

'JUST LISTEN AND DO WHAT I TELL YOU.'

'But, Boyce —'

'CLUTCH UP! HANDBRAKE OFF! PULL AWAY — AND YOU!' Boyce gives a Mondeo the finger for nosing in front of them. 'INDICATE! PULL OUT! SECOND! – YOU WOULD, WOULD YOU?'

Yanking on the handbrake, Boyce erupts from the car and assaults the Mondeo driver at the lights. Carrie gets out of the car and walks away, leaving the Golf blocking the traffic and Boyce in a chorus of beeping.

Tears run freely down her face as she stumbles through the maze of streets backing on to the wharves behind the aquarium. With no interest in fishes, or anything else except somewhere to hide, she goes in.

Wandering dully past angel fish and lion fish, Temperate Zones and the Sea Shore, Carrie has no idea how much time has passed when she finds herself locking eyes with Luke through a tank of navy genoas. A yellow jack fins between them. Luke crosses his eyes. Finally Carrie smiles.

'What are you doing here?' Luke appears round the tank.

'Running away from my driving lesson?'

'Me too.'

'Who's teaching you?'

'Diana Buchanan. First Gear Driving School.'

'What's she like?'

'She's my mum.' A slim girl slips her hand into Luke's. 'That's how we met, isn't it?'

'Jules had free tickets to the aquarium,' Luke explains.

'Right,' says Carrie.

'She lives down the road,' Luke says. 'It's just that her mum had this –'

'Seen the sharks yet?' says Carrie. 'See you later, all right?'

Some time later Luke and Juliet Buchanan loop back around to the Shark Tunnel, in the direction Carrie went, Luke pushing the pace anxiously and missing most of the fishes.

'What's the hurry?'

'Let's see the sharks,' says Luke.

'She's your ex, right?' Jules guesses.

Is that what she is, his ex? Behind him, in the Deepest Tank in Europe, giant cod glide by. Luke watches as a diver in scuba gear enters and starts a feeding frenzy by giving out little fish, as the bigger fish boil around him and a crowd gathers against the reinforced glass of the roof-high tank.

'Shark Tunnel's left round this bend,' Luke says, consulting his map.

'We haven't seen the octopus yet.' Jules shrugs off her perfectly faded denim jacket and shakes out her perfectly straightened hair. 'Ugh, it's hot in here.'

Luke moves into the Shark Tunnel, scanning the crowd, spotting Carrie at last, about to move on to the sea horses. Red and green lights play in her face as sickle-mouthed reef sharks fin by overhead and a cheesy tape plays in the tunnel: *Reef sharks and tiger sharks are among the most dangerous and unpredictable predators of the ocean* —

'Feels like *they're* looking at *us*,' Luke says, joining Carrie.

'Where did your friend go?' says Carrie, still looking up.

'Dunno.'

'Did you see the octopus?'

'Saw it before, when Danny fainted in the skate pond.'

'Didn't hurt the skates, did he?'

'Didn't improve 'em,' Luke says. 'I only just met her,' he says. 'I don't even know why I came.'

'They look horrible when they go past, don't they?' Carrie says, as a tiger shark brushes close. 'The way they roll their eyes.'

'Ben all right, then?'

'No.'

Luke puts his arm around her. Carrie shrugs him off. 'Luke, don't! There's an ugly one!' The sharks part suddenly to reveal Boyce Crocker entering the tunnel.

'You're not wrong,' Luke mutters, turning away.

Shouldering his way through the crowd like the missing link, Boyce Crocker puts his hands on his hips and confronts Carrie. 'CAR GOT TOWED – YOU HAPPY NOW?'

'Boyce – I didn't mean –'

'VOLLIE CALLED A MEET. YOU,' Boyce says, 'HOME. NOW.'

'Why isn't Luke here, again?' Danny complains over dinner at Home Sweet Home Terrace that night.

'You know he's doing a late shift,' Mum says.

'All he thinks about is money since he broke up with Carrie.'

'He broke up with Carrie?' Mum says.

'Like the way I have to look after Farty McNab while *he's* off coining it somewhere,' Danny grumbles.

'Wyndham's got his job now,' Mum says.

'I still have to *see* him, don't I?'

'I *am* here, all right?' says Wyndham.

'Are you?' says Danny. 'I never noticed.'

'Eat up, Danny,' Dad says. 'So, Wyndham — how's your father?'

'Working,' Wyndham says carefully.

'As?'

'A — steeplejack. They wouldn't give you a job at the cinema,' he says to Danny.

'Didn't know Clifford was a steeplejack,' Mum says. 'He was off work with a disability allowance when we met him ten years ago.'

'He comes from a long line of steeplejacks,' Wyndham insists, helping himself to chips.

'Is your name really Nettlefold?' Danny says, through pork chops and gravy.

'A-long-line-of-steeplejacks,' Wyndham repeats, helping himself to more gravy. 'What's so funny about Nettlefold?'

'We looked you up on the family tree,' Danny says. 'It says you were born in '85, but you aren't eighteen, are you?'

Wyndham adjusts his position to relieve himself of gas. 'What do you think?' he says.

'Not at the table, Wyndham,' says Dad.

'There's a mistake — obviously.'

'What's your brother's name?' Danny persists.

Wyndham blinks. 'Can I get the brown sauce, Auntie Cath?'

'Help yourself, Wyndham,' Mum says.

'Give you a clue, it begins with an H!' Danny shouts after him, as Wyndham leaves the room.

The front door slams and Luke looks in.

'Early tonight,' Mum says.

'Stocktaking,' Luke says. 'Wotcha, Danny.'

'Your dinner's in the oven.'

'I'm not hungry,' Luke says. 'I had a bag of chips.'

'Take a seat, you look tired,' Mum says. 'The shine's gone off you lately.'

Luke pulls out a chair and sits down. 'How d'you mean, the shine?'

Wyndham appears at the door with a bottle of HP Sauce.

'Yo, Windy,' says Luke.

'I'm sitting there,' Wyndham says.

'You were, you mean,' Luke says.

Wyndham sits on Luke's lap and takes off the top of the sauce bottle. Normally Luke would keel sideways from under him to avoid contact with the Wyndham buttocks. Now he says coldly, 'Get off.'

Wyndham dots his half-eaten chop with brown sauce.

Mum slides his plate across to her place. 'Wyndham, sit here.'

Wyndham pulls back his plate and begins dotting his chips, having to thump the bottle and put his elbow in Luke's face.

'It begins with an H,' Danny says.

'Danny, really,' Mum says.

'I'm tired, all right?' says Luke.

'Henry? Harry? Funny you can't remember the name of your own brother.'

Suddenly Luke erupts, throwing Wyndham and his HP Sauce sideways on to the two-seater kitchen settee.

'Harvey, Harold, Hugo – well?' Danny shouts, as Wyndham runs out of the room covered in gravy and chips.

'Sit down, Danny,' Mum says. 'Wyndham doesn't want to talk about Harris.'

'No!' Wyndham yells. 'I don't!' Stamping up each stair deliberately, he slams the door to his room.

'Don't wind him up,' Dad says. 'Or we'll have to ring his mother.'

'He winds me up,' Luke says.

'How old is he anyway?' says Danny.

'He's a bit immature –'

'Like Luke,' Danny says.

'– but he's doing well. Thirteen or fourteen, isn't he?'

'I gather you're not seeing Carrie,' Mum says, when the sound of the shower upstairs announces a Wyndham hygiene session.

'No,' Luke says.

'They finished,' says Danny. 'I told you.'

'She dumped him – ha, ha!' shouts Wyndham.

'How can he hear?' Luke says.

'I'm not in the shower yet. I can hear if you're talking about me!' Wyndham shouts down the stairs.

Luke rushes out to get him, in time to hear the bathroom door slam and the bolt on the door shoot home.

'I saw her this afternoon!' Luke shouts up the stairs, as

though the words are being wrenched from his heart. 'No one dumped anyone – that interesting enough for you?'

'Funny how some people can't remember the name of their brothers,' Danny says later, in Wyndham's room. 'See this, Luke? That is your name, isn't it?'

'The name-tag in these pyjamas says "Barnard Walsh",' Luke whispers.

'It says "Barnard Walsh" in his bag too,' says Danny. 'Not coming out yet, is he?'

'I can't believe he's in there again.' Luke listens at the bathroom door. 'Nah, we've got ages, he's doing his whole skin-cleansing thing.'

Moments before, Wyndham's holdall had disclosed a pile of Danny's CDs. Now a mysterious lump wrapped in tissue paper appears at the bottom under a pile of deeply sad clothes. Danny tweaks its wrapper and out on to the floor bonks an object they know very well.

'Omigod,' Danny breathes.

'Can't believe he was going to nick it,' Luke says, handling it reverently and catching its bitter smell. 'Grandpa's meerschaum pipe.'

The pipe, shaped like a man's head wearing a turban, was an object you asked to look at. Meerschaum was a kind of clay found in Turkey, Dad explained, after he'd looked it up in the dictionary.

The Turk's-head pipe lived in a specially shaped satin-lined case, which had sat in the back of the left-hand drawer in the living-room sideboard, along with the best serviettes and some old silver spoons, for as long as Luke and Danny could remember. No one had seen Grandpa smoking it, because Grandpa had died from a haemorrhage, or in a lifeboat, or both − Luke could never remember which − when Luke's father was ten.

Luke had longed when he was small to see wreaths of blue smoke curling from the top of the Turk's turban. Its bowl smelled of bitter and manly things, like creaking ships and rum and the sea and the Orient beyond it, wherever the Orient was, and its stem was of honey-coloured amber, which Dad said came from Russia. It was the only thing he had of his father's, which made it special in more ways than one.

Danny had dropped the Turk recently and rattled his turban, and Dad had taken him out to the shed and introduced some Superglue into a small crack and left him clamped in a vice. *Now here he was, in Wyndham's bag −*

'Enjoying ourselves, are we?' says Wyndham, flipping on the light. 'What are you doing in my room?'

'Finding out who you are,' says Danny. 'You're not Cousin Wyndham, are you?'

'Who says?'

'Try Barnard Walsh,' says Luke. 'You've been robbing his things.'

'Not very nice, is it, going through someone's room?'

'Neither is stealing Dad's pipe − or my CDs,' says Danny.

'I'm borrowing them to clone them,' says Wyndham. 'And I'm looking after the pipe.'

'Yeah, right . . . Drop the act, why don't you?'

'I will if you will,' says Wyndham, falling on Danny.

Danny pounds Wyndham's chest and kicks Wyndham's back, while Luke applies a headlock. Wyndham topples sideways, taking Luke with him, while Danny scrambles for a purchase over Wyndham's legs with both of his. Luke sits on Wyndham's head.

'You're catching the next train home. What are you catching?'

'A flea off your bum!' Wyndham squeaks defiantly.

'Ask him who he is,' Danny says.

'You're not Wyndham Nettlenuts, are you —'

'Luke, is Wyndham there?' Mum shouts up the stairs. 'What's all that bumping about?'

Wyndham uses the moment to free his head. 'I'm up here, Auntie Cath! Your dad asked me to take the pipe to the repair shop, in case you're interested,' he adds to Luke and Danny in a furious undertone.

'Liar,' says Luke.

'Striped pyjamas,' says Danny.

'Who's Barnard Walsh?' says Luke.

'Let me up or I'll chuck.' Wyndham coughs threateningly.

'Poor old Barnard Walsh, he must be getting cold, walking around with no clothes on,' says Danny.

Mrs Couch looks round the door. 'Nice to see you all getting along. Wyndham, your mum's on the phone.'

Wyndham throws Luke off. 'And don't try anything while I'm gone.'

Danny follows him to eavesdrop. The minute he's alone, Luke stuffs everything he can find of Wyndham's – or Barnard's – into Wyndham's – or Barnard's – plaid holdall. He bumps the holdall downstairs and lodges it by the front door. 'Anything?' he signals to Danny, listening outside the living-room door.

'No, Mum, I'm fine,' Wyndham says loudly. 'Harris is all right, is he? I might need a bit of CASH. Yes, I'm RUNNING SHORT. AUNTIE CATH MIGHT HELP ME IF I ASK HER NICELY –'

Danny punts the door shut and follows Luke into the kitchen.

'I think Marion must have a cold,' his mother's reporting. 'I couldn't hear what she was saying all that well –'

'It's possible,' says Luke's father, over the telly.

Concerns for missing thirteen-year-old Julian Coombes have been partially allayed, the newsreader announces, *since his mother contacted Social Services. A spokesman said that the call was indistinct: 'I couldn't hear what she was saying –'*

'Dad, did you ask Wyndham to take Grandpa's pipe to the repair shop?' Danny bursts out.

'What?'

'Did you ask Wyndham to take Grandpa's pipe to the repair shop?'

'Mum says thanks for everything. If I could have a little allowance every week, she says she'll send you a cheque, and it'd help me save up for my school uniform,' Wyndham says virtuously, appearing at the kitchen door.

'You have to buy your own *uniform*?' Luke boggles.

'And some Ben and Jerry's would be nice, whenever you remember.'

'She sounds a bit poorly,' Mum says. 'Did you tell her about your job?'

'I told her everything,' Wyndham says, smiling and going out.

Danny gets the blender and makes up a milk shake with chocolate syrup, banana and a whole pint of milk and downs the lot in a rage.

'Now then, Danny,' Mum says. 'Did you check your diet sheet?'

'Keeping my sugar levels up,' Danny says, wiping his mouth.

Later Dad opens the sideboard drawer and takes out a familiar-looking case. 'This pipe, you mean?' he says to Danny, displaying the Turk's head inside.

'I thought it was out in the shed.'

'It was. I brought it in.'

'That doesn't mean anything,' Danny rages. 'He's put it back, can't you *see*?'

'Who has?'

'Wyndham. He had it in his holdall.'

'Looking at it probably,' Dad says. 'I said he could take it out whenever he wanted to. We had a talk about dads, you see – this pipe reminds me of mine.'

'He was stealing it.'

'I don't think so.'

'Speak to Auntie Marion.'

'Again?'

As Danny rages at Dad, upstairs Luke decides to have a quiet word with Wyndham. 'You're leaving, all right? Tonight,' Luke says, hefting Wyndham's back against the wall. He *had* seemed all right, just a bit of a loser, but nicking stuff is way out of line. 'You crossed the line, all right? I'm not going to just stand by while you make a monkey out of my family –'

'Wouldn't that be monkeys?' Wyndham says.

For a moment Luke considers hitting him. 'I'm taking your bag to the station. You might want to get down there soon. They blow up unattended luggage.'

6. Hang or Drown

'I never thought it would end this way.' That was what Ben told me. 'I never dreamed there'd be so much to pay.'

'It wasn't your fault,' I told him. 'It had nothing to do with you at the end of the day. It was about some stupid casino wars. It said so in the paper.'

'They were after me for the motor,' he said. 'I should've stayed away.'

He wanted out, after that. But whenever Ben tried to escape, Vollie wouldn't let him. 'Families muck in together,' he said. 'There's work here. Family work. You don't want to go off your head.'

'Si said I was clever,' Ben said, 'that wasting it's a crime. I want to go to college. I want to do it for Si.'

'A crime,' said Vollie, 'that's a laugh. Shut up and graft. You're a Crocker.'

Ben's lost it now. He drove an N-reg Astra up the back of a van in a car chase and legged it across Central Park and through the Palisades Shopping Mall before he got away.

I hope he's learned a lesson. I talked to him about it, but none of it seems to stick — maybe because I'm not straight with him, because I'm not being straight with myself, because I don't want to see what he's doing. I'm not being straight with myself because then I'll have to look at my family and see the damage, not only to them, but to me . . .

The damage to Ben's the worst. After the Lucky Strike, he'll do anything anyone asks him to. He doesn't care any more. Not now that Si's gone.

— Confessions of Carmen Crocker

Funny how things happen. On his way to the station to dump Wyndham's stupid plaid holdall Luke pauses outside the house he'd thought might be Carrie's the other night, when suddenly the door opens and Vollie cranes out. 'What?'

Luke opens and closes his mouth. 'I —'

Vollie looks down at the holdall. 'Cousin Louis, is it?'

'Um,' Luke says gratefully. 'Is Carrie — Carmen in?'

Vollie sniffs him. 'She is, as it goes. All right,' he says, 'get in.'

Beyond the bicycle in the corridor a kitchen filled with frying smells opens out. Carrie spins round as they enter, spatula in hand over a spitting frying pan. 'Lu —'

'Louis, Cousin Louis, remember me?' Luke hugs her closely and tips her a wink as they part.

'Louis made it after all,' says Vollie, getting his legs back under a mixed grill. 'Stick your bag in the corner,' he says to Luke.

Carrie hacks an egg out of the frying pan, misses a plate and drops it on to the floor.

Vollie narrows his eyes. 'Make a pigging mess. What's the matter with you?'

'Let me get that,' Luke offers, fetching a cloth from the sink.

'I'd hardly've recognized you, Louis,' Carrie says, as their eyes meet.

'Hasn't been *that* long, has it?' Luke chances.

'Since the lockets,' says Carrie. 'When Uncle Louis gave us all pictures of the family to remind us we're Crockers?'

'Thought Louis was your cousin, not your uncle,' says Luke unguardedly.

'You are,' says Carrie simply. 'Your dad's called Louis too.'

'He knows who his father is,' Vollie says. 'Know who your father is, don't you?'

'NOT LIKE SOME,' Boyce bellows through from the living room.

'You're a lot bigger than the last time I saw you, Carmen,' Luke says. He can feel Vollie's eyes on him. 'How old are you now anyway?'

'Almost seventeen,' says Carrie evenly. She won't give him away.

A bull terrier bats in through a dog flap and stiffens instantly.

'Stow it, Jeeves,' says Vollie, throwing a sock in its face. He gets up and takes Luke's coat and shoves it at the dog's nose. 'He's got the Crocker scent now. You won't have no trouble from him.'

Jeeves rumbles at 'Louis' and lifts the sides of his mouth.

'Jeevesie, don't,' says Carrie, taking a dog biscuit from the bowl on the floor and tossing it to him.

Jeevesie jumps up and bags it with a resounding snap.

'He got out the other day and bit some bint in the street, but they never had any witnesses,' Vollie sneers. 'Like to see them get some.'

'You should keep him in, he's dangerous.' A boy of about Luke's age appears at the door. 'Cousin Louis, is it?'

'Yo,' says Luke, wishing he hadn't.

'I greet you with the sign of the Crockers,' says the boy from the locket photo sardonically, putting two Vs to his forehead to make a W for 'Winners'. 'Don't remember you, I'm afraid.'

'Got a job for you, Benny-boy – Project Louis, all right?' says Vollie, pulling them together into his cold personal space with an arm around each of them. 'Ben shows Louis a thing or two. Louis takes care of business, while Benny-boy cools off. All right with you, Louis?'

'What business – used cars?' says Cousin Louis.

'Used cars, yeah, that's right.'

Jeevesie moistens his chops and trembles with the desire to take a chunk out of Luke.

'If you think I'll be useful,' says Cousin Louis.

'Carmen,' says Vollie, 'make Louis some bacon and eggs.'

'Louis' sits beside Carmen and watches telly the rest of the evening. Stealing kisses from Carrie while Boyce snores after Ben and Vollie go out is never going to get him anything but a dig in the ribs, but Louis is prepared to risk it. When at last she shows him up to bed, Carrie melts a little. 'Not here – next door.' Putting her hand over Luke's face, she steers him laughingly out of her room and into the next one. 'You're my cousin, all right? You're in here with Ben, except he's gone out on a job.'

'What sort of job?' Luke says, eyeing the bunk beds.

'Thanks for this – for being here. It's dangerous. What are you *doing*, being Louis?'

'Vollie's mistake, I just went with it.'

'And anyway, things aren't so bad. At least –'

'Where is he?'

'Who?'

'The real Louis.'

'You're all right,' Carrie says. 'He probably couldn't make it, Vollie said. I –'

'What?'

'I think he's learned his lesson. Ben crashed another car, but I think he's going to stop.'

'Go to bed,' Luke says, visions of helping her again, like he did when she was sick, making him want to be as strong as she thinks he is. 'I'll see you in the morning, yeah?'

Carrie nods and kisses him and spends thirty-five minutes in the bathroom. Luke wanders into her room again, the room he's only imagined, but never seen before. It's surprisingly plain, with few ornaments – few possessions of any kind. Open on the bed is a notebook titled *Confessions* in a neat but looping hand. The last entry was a few days ago. *The damage to Ben's the worst*, Luke reads. *After the Lucky Strike, he'll do anything anyone asks him to. He doesn't care any more. Not now that Si's gone.*

What's Ben Crocker like? He doesn't look like a crim. He

seems pretty cool, Luke thinks. But then Wyndham looks like butter wouldn't melt when he's mad as a bag of snakes. Annoying not to have dumped his holdall at the station, but then some things are more important than some gassy klepto at home . . .

Luke rings home at eleven from Ben Crocker's room at The Crock. 'Mum? I'm sleeping over at Michael's. Michael Bowden. Bow-den. Behind the fish factory, yeah? I came back to his after snooker club . . . I'm whispering because he's asleep. Work tomorrow, yeah . . . Can you get my overall out of the washing machine? Leave it over a chair. I'll look in and pick it up, yeah?'

Setting his mobile to 'alarm', 'Louis' settles down in the bunk which he hopes isn't Ben's and in moments his thoughts swim away, as if the effort of being Cousin Louis uses up calories or brain tissue or some more mysterious energy.

Carrie listens next door and smiles – What is he like?

Luke turns over in bed, his brain scintillating with plans and seething with helpful feelings, when a shark with Boyce's head swims up and asks him, 'WHAT ARE YOU DOING?' and 'WHO DO YOU THINK YOU ARE?' And as he turns and pitches in his dreams on the inside, at last, of that wall which for so long has kept him out of The Crock, Luke Couch dreams of netting that shark and chopping it into pieces.

'Haven't I seen you around?' Vollie asks Luke next morning, over yet another mixed grill.

'Louis' laughs carelessly. 'Maybe I've got a twin.'

'Somewhere with patio furniture, wasn't it?'

'Where's Ben?' Luke gets up and washes his plate. *Please God, let him not connect kitchen taps or plumbing fittings with the day he saw me at Make It All.*

'Checking the car, how do I know?' says Vollie, scanning page three and forgetting Louis exists.

Backing out of the kitchen through a snowfall of white hats from a clothes-drying rack, 'Louis' finds Ben Crocker outside, examining the Golf GTi with a ding in it parked carelessly in front of The Crock.

'So you move up and down the row,' Luke says. 'No fixed abode, yeah?'

'That's just a stupid story,' Ben says. 'We moved a couple of times.'

'Right,' Luke says, 'but I thought –'

'People say all sorts of things. You should know, you're a Crocker.'

'This your motor?' says Luke.

'What does it look like?' Ben says, bending to examine the ding in its side.

'Me and my brother saw this Golf GTi being stolen –'

'Didn't know you had a brother.'

'Yeah,' Luke says. 'He's called Danny. He's pretty immature.'

'How old is he?'

'A baby,' 'Louis' chances, wondering if he can cover this.

'Would be, then, wouldn't he? Carmen,' Ben decides.

'Must've dinged the car having driving lessons with Boyce. Want to take her out?'

'Carmen?'

'Get in the car,' says Ben Crocker.

'It's locked,' Luke says.

'Down to you to open it.'

'Keys?' Luke says.

'Don't know anything, do you?' Ben produces a screwdriver from his jacket and twists it into the lock. He gets in and unlocks the passenger door for Luke. Luke watches while Ben pops a section of plastic off the steering column. It comes away easily, as though it's been popped before. 'Bypass the ignition switch by joining these wires.' Ben demonstrates which ones and the engine thrums to life. 'It's OK, but you have to work fast, and you have to know what you're doing. Easier to fish for keys. No one does hot-wiring now, unless they have to.'

'Why would you need to?' says Luke. 'If you're dealing in used cars, you've got the keys to them, right?'

Ben dangles the keys at him. 'Right.'

'I heard you went joyriding. Out to the Drome.'

'That what you heard?'

'It's all over town.'

'Stupid stories, I told you.'

'Not what Carrie says.'

'I told him I'd stopped all that.' Ben breaks off, looking out of the window. 'Si said I had to stay clean if I hung around at the casino. He didn't mind at first, then he said he'd lose his job if I got a rep —'

'You're all right to pull away,' Luke says, automatically checking the mirrors.

'I'm not driving, you are,' Ben says. 'Swap places, all right?'

Luke checks his mirror ten times before he pulls away. 'You know I'm a learner, right? I should have "L" plates up.'

'I'll overlook it this time,' says Ben, popping in a wad of gum. 'Go down Commercial Road and out on the Leyton Way.'

Luke changes up into third as the Golf shudders over the cobbles. 'Which way at the end of the street?'

'I *was* staying clean-ish, but then I got in with some characters,' Ben says, ignoring him. 'Right, then left – keep in the middle lane on Commercial Road. Before, it was just kid's stuff. They gave me a set of keys and paid me 200 quid to reverse this Merc out of someone's drive at six o'clock in the morning. So I'm walking through this estate, birds are singing and stuff, everyone's asleep behind their curtains, when I finally get to the house – Go right on the Parkway here.'

Luke pulls down a slip road and merges nervously.

'So there's the motor in the driveway. There's a milk float going round the estate and the sun's coming up over the houses and everything's peaceful and stuff – and there's this kid's bike in their front garden –' Ben breaks off and looks out of the window. 'In the end I threw the keys in the hedge and took off. Some story got around that I'd smacked it up, but I never even stole the Merc. It got back to *them*, of course. I knew they'd come after me. They thought I worked at the casino. They weren't going to let me make fools of them. Si said, Tell the police, like that was going to stop them finding me. Si thought he'd lose his job, but in the end, you know what, he lost his life.'

'"Casino Wars" or something,' Luke says. 'That's what it said in the paper.'

'Simon Bradshaw, assistant floor manager at the Lucky Strike,' Ben says proudly. 'A lot of responsibility with that – not bad for a Barnard Walsh boy.'

'A what boy?' Luke says. *That name again.*

'Barnard Walsh, Hermione Griffiths, Talbot King, James Fielding-Knight, not so bright – all the blocks had names. Me 'n' Si were in Barnard Walsh, till Vollie got me out. "Barnard Walsh Forever," we had to say when we played soccer against other blocks – worst stinking rat-hole you ever saw in your life, and that was just the people. Simon looked after me when the others pushed me around. He wasn't hard, but he was the eldest –'

'Wait,' says Luke. 'Barnard Walsh is a children's home?'

'Know someone who went there, do you?'

Luke's mind races. 'Why were you in a home?'

'What, you don't know your aunt died? Didn't your dad tell you anything? Pull off at the next services. We need petrol.'

'This exit?' says Luke. 'So did you have geeky PJs with name-tags saying "Barnard Walsh"?'

'Everything said "Barnard Walsh",' Ben says. 'Si could put up with it. Si could put up with anything. He put up with me, the system, anything they threw at him, and he could still be cool with it. He was patient that way. He knew he'd get out one day. Me, I couldn't see it. I didn't think anyone cared –'

'My driving instructor's bringing me out on the Parkway soon as I get stopping at junctions right,' says Luke. 'I can stop at junctions all right, but I went over this roundabout once. Diana Buchanan, First Gear Driving School? She goes *mad* if you don't indicate.'

'Never learned, myself,' Ben says carelessly. 'Pull in here. I'll fill up.'

Checking his mirror ostentatiously and indicating like mad, Luke pulls in at Parkway Services. 'My side or yours?'

'What?'

'The filler cap.'

'I can't remember, can I?' Ben says. 'Stick it as tight as you can behind that Vectra.'

Luke parks snugly behind a Vectra waiting at the next pump. Stickers on the tops of the petrol guns read: 'Car Criminals Fill up Here Too. Lock Your Car.'

Ben ducks out of the Golf. 'Keep the engine running, all right?'

'You're supposed to turn off,' Luke says.

'Keep your foot on the accelerator. See those security cameras?'

Luke sees them. 'So?'

'We've parked close up to the car in front, plus our rear plates are dirty –'

'Think they sell Haribo Mix here?' says Luke.

'What are you, a kid? I'm showing you stuff here, all right?'

What stuff, Luke wonders, watching Ben fill up. He'd be a right nutter to work with – Ben had issues like Wyndham had hot dogs . . .

Ben hangs up the petrol gun and takes a hike to the Gents. Luke's just wondering if there's a back entrance to the filling-station stores, where Ben must be inside paying, when he spots Ben in his mirrors, sprinting back to the car with his collar turned up.

Ben throws himself into the passenger seat. 'Drive, as you're a Crocker!'

Luckily the Vectra's gone and the exit's clear. Luke revs and almost stalls, but finally speeds away. 'That was quick. What's the hurry?'

Ben sorts out his collar. 'Be surprised if they got our number.'

'What did we just do?' Luke says. 'Did we fill up without paying?'

'Quick, aren't you?' says Ben. 'Big chain. They can afford it.'

A cold feeling grips Luke's heart. Without asking Ben, he takes the next roundabout all the way around and points the Golf back towards the filling station. Suddenly Ben grabs the handbrake, Luke fighting for control as the car spins through 180 degrees in the middle of the road, to stall in the opposite direction.

'Take it away,' Ben says.

'Smooth,' says Luke sardonically. 'They'll never notice us now.'

'Start up and drive,' says Ben.

Luke starts up and pulls away again, the words *mirrors, signal, manoeuvre* seeming to belong to some other world where people do what they should. The adrenalin really pumping now, he accelerates on the Parkway and tries to control his voice. 'Often do this, do you?'

'Don't say you didn't enjoy it,' Ben grins, putting a fist through the sunroof.

'You'll get done for it, sooner or later.'

'Who cares?' Ben says.

'Me, for starters. And Si.'

Ben glances across. 'What d'*you* know about Si?'

'Carmen showed me her diary,' Luke lies. 'She thinks you're going to blow it now Simon isn't around.'

'Drive faster,' Ben says harshly.

'Simon wanted you to stop joyriding before you copped it.'

'Shut up about Si and drive,' Ben says.

'Police Speed Check Area,' Luke warns. 'There's an unmarked car behind us.'

'Pig on our back, is there?'

'We could be in trouble unless —'

Ben lunges over Luke's leg, forcing down Luke's foot on the accelerator, topping out at eighty as Luke fights to stay on the road.

'Floor it!' Ben shouts. '*Hang or drown! What does it matter?*'

*

'What was *that* about?' Luke says, when at last the approach to the Willey's Industrial Estate roundabout forces them into a queue. 'You're a nutter. I'm out of here soon as we get off the Parkway. I thought we were dog meat, then. Cops weren't chasing us anyway.'

'Hang or drown, get done for speeding or thieving, what's the diff?'

Luke puts his head on the steering wheel. 'What's that supposed to mean?'

'This book at the home, *Kidnapped*,' Ben says after a moment. It had this map on the front − "Wreck of the Brig *Covenant*, and the Probable Course of David Balfour's Wanderings". I used to lie in bed at Barnard Walsh and look at that map and wonder what *wandering* was like.'

The queue moves slowly forwards. 'What happens in it?' Luke says at last.

'These redcoats are after David and Alan Breck Stewart − they get framed for topping this Red Fox bloke? So they reach this raging river. It turns David's guts to water. Alan jumps to this rock in the middle. Come on, he goes. You can do it. David jumps, but then he's stuck. He can't go any further. If he stays, the redcoats'll get him. He's just stuck on this rock with the river roaring around him −'

'Might as well jump.'

'He can't swim. Old Alan Breck, he gives David this tot of brandy, then he shouts, "Hang or drown!" You've read it, right? You're named after him.'

'Who?'

'Stevenson, Robert Louis?'

'I'm getting out at the next lay-by. You're on your own,' 'Louis' says.

'Relax,' Ben says. 'We're going home. Pull in at Willey Park Garage. Vollie said buy some milk.'

Luke pulls in at the garage. 'Where do I put it?'

'Behind that Audi,' Ben says, watching the bloke in the Audi pop open his filler cap from inside the car and fill up with no keys in his hand.

'So, did he make it?'

'Who?'

'David Balfour?' Luke asks.

'He made it,' Ben says. 'I didn't.'

Sticking his gum on the dash, he watches the Audi owner head into the shop to pay.

'Are you getting milk or what?' Luke says. 'What are we –'

'Get ready, all right?' Ben gets out of the car.

'What for?'

'Go home the long way round,' he tells Luke rapidly through the window, fishing a white hat from his pocket and jamming it on Luke's head. 'No one'll bother you now. Mine's an Audi. Drive on.'

'What are you –'

Ben jumps into the Audi, turns the key still handily in the ignition and drives it squealing off the forecourt. Luke starts the Golf and puts down his foot, 'Go home the long way round' hammering inside his head like the only thing left to hold on to, that and *not losing Ben*.

Driving on automatic pilot, hardly knowing what he's

doing, hardly able to steer with the stinging sweat in his eyes and the throbbing pulse in his chest jumping into his throat, Luke guns the Golf after the Audi. As they ride the ramp to the Leyton Way, Ben's triumphant fist appears through the Audi's window.

Double-tracking back across town some time later, really quite enjoying himself, answering Ben's thumbs-up before peeling off the Leyton Way on to Commercial Road, 'Louis' has time to check out the cool white Koolaroo hat in his mirror before he slips on his shades and hits 'play' on a *Summer Mix* CD.

Catching grief from Mason Greaves at Make It All or being a member of the White Hats, for whom other cars melt away on roundabouts and the toll on the bridge is waived, which would be more fun?

Not much doubt about *that* one. Still buzzing from the drive up the Parkway, not even the mid-morning silence back at The Crock bursts Cousin Louis's bubble. Opening a wad of Ben's gum, he parks up carefully and assesses the mood.

Ben'll be back before long, probably after another detour around the town. Meanwhile, he, 'Louis', can be siphoning off the morning's haul of petrol into the containers stacked in the garden. Funny how, somehow, he'd known what they were for.

7. Drown

Driving illegally, stealing petrol, aiding and abetting car theft . . . next morning the list of things he'd done wrong beats in Luke's head like a hammer. Cousin Louis hadn't stolen anything, but he'd stood by while someone else had. Kiss goodbye to college if the CCTV at Willey Park had caught a full-face shot as he caned the Golf off the forecourt . . .

Surprised to find himself in his own room at Home Sweet Home Terrace, Luke gets up for work like a zombie. He rubs his face in the mirror. *The Audi bloke's face at Willey Park as Ben leathered off in his car* . . .

Where had his head been at? All the previous day he'd felt like someone else. Vollie had sat unnervingly close over a Five-Stack Fry Up at teatime. Still Ben hadn't come home.

'Big morning, coz?'

'What?' Luke had looked up over his sausages, the elation he'd felt that morning wearing thin already. What was he doing here?

'Ben show you a thing or two?'

Ben's fist through the sunroof. The freedom of the road. 'Yeah,'

Cousin Louis said guardedly. 'He showed me a thing or two.'

'Show you something else.' Vollie had mapped out the manor using cutlery and lottery tickets. The salt and pepper represented the gasholders. Vollie outlined his plans for a pincer movement enclosing those businesses that Wouldn't Give Him The Time Of Day with Those That Owed Him Big Time. 'Then we can put in the squeeze, see?'

Cousin Louis saw. But Vollie's gimlet eyes seemed to bore right through him.

Later, he'd talked with Carrie in her room. 'Ben and me did some stuff today.'

Carrie had looked up sharply over the *Confessions*. 'What kind of stuff?'

'Ben nicked an Audi from Willey Park Garage. He drove off in it somewhere.'

'But he's on probation.'

'Tell him that.'

Carrie put down her pen and covered her face. 'Where's he gone? The Drome?'

'How do I know?'

'What about you?'

'Hopefully I won't get done and blow my chance at college. Tell Vollie I'm out on a job. I've got to go home,' Luke said. 'This Louis thing's doing my head in.'

Carrie had crossed the room to be with him. 'Stay with me, Luke, will you?'

'You knew what Ben was like –'

'So did you.'

'Why can't you be straight about anything?'

'My diary isn't enough? I know you've been reading it.'

'Only because it was open.'

'Leave it, Luke, all right? You don't know anything about us. Don't come in my room again.'

Luke had gone out.

'Wait! What job?' Carrie had come to the door.

'I'm supposed to collect a BMW for Boyce and park it near the Albert gasholder.'

'It'll be paid for. What's your problem?'

'What do you think?' Luke had said coldly, watching himself hurt her and going into his room and shutting the door.

He'd slipped out later that night and walked home under the gasholders, feeling the 'Cousin Louis' persona slide off him with every step nearer normality and Home Sweet Home Terrace. Even the sound of Wyndham babbling in his sleep as he'd let himself in had seemed like a welcome-home.

He'd found a note on the kitchen table: 'Mason Greaves rang. I rang Michael Bowden's house and he said you were on your way home. What's going on? Love, Mum. PS Sausages in mike.'

Luke keys 'messages' on his phone. Sure enough, Bowden had rung: 'Dunno what's going down but I covered for you anyway. Be home tonight or be rotten with your mum. Later, Bowden.'

So Bowden comes through – the boy with the bat-ears at snooker club, an unlikely candidate for New Best Mate but clearly gold in an emergency, noses ahead of the pack . . .

Sandwiching two cold sausages inside a wedge of bread, Luke climbs the stairs and looks in on Wyndham. 'Still here, Farty McNab?'

Wyndham sits bolt upright in bed. 'Frankenstein, is thad you?'

'Shut up, you div, it's me,' Luke says, entering the room.

Wyndham might be dreaming but he certainly hasn't been asleep to the advantages of his, Luke's, not being at home. Familiar-looking stuff covers the floor. Luke's CDs spill off a chair. His computer sits on a desk, covered in his – Luke's – clothes.

'See you took all my stuff.'

'Izza-what?' Wyndham says, rubbing his head.

'Couldn't wait to nick all my things, then,' Luke says again. 'D'you come from a children's home or what?'

'Dunno what you mean,' Wyndham says, fully awake at last. 'You took all my stuff. What am I supposed to wear?'

Forced to live out of Wyndham's holdall for the last couple of days, Luke's actually wearing Wyndham's pants, but the horror of this remains nameless.

'Your stuff says "Barnard Walsh". Barnard Walsh is a children's home. I know you're not Cousin Wyndham.'

'My bag got mixed up with someone else's on the train.' Wyndham watches Luke. 'Ring my mum if you don't believe me.'

'I might ring your mum tomorrow,' says Luke. 'And you can give my telly back.'

'Auntie Cath said I could borrow it –'

'Tomorrow,' Luke says, slamming out.

Realizing with horror that a lot of the stuff he's wearing has a *Barnard Walsh name-tag* in it, Luke throws off his clothes in his plundered room and wonders who he is.

Things get muddled pretty easily. Could there be some explanation? Wyndham isn't eighteen, like the family tree says he should be, but can there be some mistake? After all, if *he'd* got knocked down and taken to hospital on the way here, quite apart from them seeing the pants (don't even go there), he, Luke Couch, might have been put down as Barnard Walsh. He's been Cousin Louis for two days. Is all this changing identities messing with his mind? Could Farty McNab next door still somehow *be* Cousin Wyndham?

In bed in the old grey T-shirt which usually stops the window rattling, curiously missed by Wyndham but at least his own, Luke stews over Make It All and the early call to Greavesie he'd have to make next morning: 'Where was I yesterday? Didn't Mum say I threw up? Yeah, I was at a mate's house. Puked all down the stairs.'

Greavesie had it in for him anyway. Too much yakking to customers, not enough time stacking MDF and PVC replacement windows . . .

The events of the day crowd in on him again as Luke turns over under the skimpy duvet kindly left to him by Wyndham. How many security cameras had been trained on them at Parkway Services? How many at Willey Park Garage?

See those security cameras? Ben had pointed out two of them.

The white hat at the second garage . . . how much of his face had it covered? Pray the two halves of his life never actually meet. Ben's two halves had met already on course for self-destruct. 'Good' Ben and 'Evil' Ben were wrestling for the wheel and one of them was winning. Ben was on the edge. Hang or drown? He'll do both, yet he isn't so different from anyone else Luke knows, himself included. How easy is it to make a mistake, to cross over to a side you didn't mean to, get some kind of *label* put on you that stops you from being able to change? Driving a hot car with the road unfolding in front of you, not caring about anything else *whatever* this moment costs you – you'd have to be dead not to thrill to it – wouldn't you? Or would you just have to have nothing *else* going down in your life? What would it take to cross over? Supposing you came from a home with a ripped settee and a rented telly in the living room and nothing else, where your family could choose between food or car insurance? Supposing breaking the rules *wasn't a choice?*

Living a double life seems a doddle in comparison. Luke finds the white hat Ben gave him and puts it on in bed. A Ben Crocker lookalike in an old grey T-shirt looks crookedly back at him from his wardrobe mirror. Luke makes the sign of the Crockers and the lookalike makes it back at him. *Luke Couch has left the building* . . .

Luke settles down in bed. He's been away what seems like ages. Meanwhile, the worm Wyndham lies coiled at the heart of his family. Levering him out seems like too much trouble. Holidays're almost over. Easier to let it go now he,

Luke, can blow the whistle on the gasman any time he gets frisky . . . Too much going down . . . Being stuck on a rock in the middle of a river'd be easy by comparison . . . *Drowning'd* be a lot simpler . . .

Annoyed with himself for stressing so long, Luke falls asleep while the window rattles and Wyndham sobs next door with the Turk's-head pipe in his hand.

Next day Mason Greaves is in a mood with Luke. 'I don't care,' he says. 'You could have called in sick yesterday morning. I could've got Granville in.'

In the still hours of a mid-week afternoon Luke dozes in Roofing & Paints, the smell of plastic sealant and creosote reminding him somehow of premium unleaded, the niff at the petrol pumps *as Ben sprints around the side of the car, turning his collar up* —

'You're not much use to me asleep on your feet. It's four forty-five. Go home.'

Luke opens his eyes and Mason Greaves swims into focus. Behind him, Make It All floods back, together with the guilt. *Hang or drown.* 'What?'

'Good night, last night, was it?'

'Told you, I was ill,' Luke mumbles.

'Get off home and be here at eight thirty tomorrow. You're either yakking or piking off lately. I've got a pile of job applications on my desk. Three days to pick it up, Luke, or collect your cards.'

'That's not fair. I'm good,' Luke says.

'Not as good as you think you are.'

If Ben sells the petrol we nicked, half the take'll be mine. And if I take my half of the take, then I'll've stolen something —

'You're doing it again.'

'Sorry,' says Luke, opening his eyes.

'What's the matter with you lately?'

'My brother's ill. He's keeping me awake,' Luke lies spontaneously.

Luke goes home via the Commercial Road chippie, and the overcooked chips and the early-evening air wake him up but don't lift the guilt, which sits on him like a goblin and weighs him down like a brick on his heart — and he'll have to live with it now. The gasholders know it, Muscles Gym knows it, the Achilles Bar and the Multiplex — even the cobbles on the street — know that something's different, that he isn't the same Luke Couch . . .

Once home, he marches into Wyndham's room and takes back his telly and watches it in his bedroom until teatime, with his arms folded tightly and his chin on his chest.

Over dinner, when his mother says, 'That's a nice jumper, Wyndham — Luke's got a jumper like that, haven't you, Luke?' he wipes ketchup venomously up and down Wyndham's sweater, which for some reason he's still wearing, and spits, 'That *is* my jumper,' and says nothing else the rest of the evening.

When Danny takes him aside and tells him how he found Wyndham packing to leave and how he — Danny — actually stopped him, Luke looks at him incredulously.

'I know,' Danny says, 'but he's all right, just a bit

annoying sometimes. And he had this pipe tobacco – Can you believe he was going to smoke Grandpa's *pipe* before he left? "You'll smoke out the room or puke," I said. "You'll set the house on fire. I've had loads of accidents. I dropped a Busy Lizzie down the toilet once –"'

Luke pushes past wearily.

'"Dad'll find out," I said,' Danny goes on, round the side of Luke's bedroom door. 'I told him, and then he went quiet –'

Luke shuts the door and flips on the telly. Later he wakes up from a doze in which a giant Mason Greaves is making him eat a can of paint, to find his mobile buzzing. 'Yeah?'

'Luke, can you come over, I –'

'Carrie? Are you OK?'

'I'm all right, it's just –'

'I'm on my way,' Luke says, wide awake in an instant.

Under the shadows of the Vicky and the Albert, past the Multiplex car park, already choked with Saturday-night cinemagoers, Luke slips silently towards Carrie's house. Beneath him the lights of the Achilles Bar pulse purple and pink on the tarmac. Groups of clubbers form outside Goss Bowl and Big Burger, one bunch including Bowden.

'Couch, what gives?' he shouts up, spotting Luke's head over the wall.

'Naff all. You?' Luke shouts back without pausing, ruthlessly deleting text messages from his phone as he goes. *Luke its Julie why not reply 4 a change?* Delete. *Luke – Jules. Party at mine this Sat.* Delete. *What did I do, love Juliet?* Delete.

'We're going up Minsters, then Zanzibar!' Bowden shouts through cupped hands, naming a cheesy bar and a tweenies disco. 'Luke! You up for it?'

'No way!' Luke hurries on, following the brick wall behind the cinema car park as cars beep angrily below, searching for a place to park before the nine o'clock screenings.

Right on to Gashouse Lane, left down Standish Ope. The Crock shines under the moon. Carrie's pale face lights her window. Appearing like a ghost at the door, she wafts Luke up to the top step of the stairs, past the raised voices in the living room: 'YOU TOTALLED AN AUDI?'

'I heard a siren and I panicked, all right?'

'AND THERE'S THAT BMW –'

'Shut it, Boyce.'

'They were after me, Vollie, I swear.'

'I could've put it on ice in the Albert, couldn't I, if you hadn't gone off your head?'

'Can't get it back now, can I? What d'you want me to do?'

'WENT AND TORCHED IT, DID YOU?'

'Benny-boy's upset. Oh, Si, I miss you, come back –'

'Shut up about Si, you –'

The sound of furniture being turned over. Luke takes Carrie's hand. Like ten-year-olds listening on the top step of the stairs to their parents' rowing, hoping against hope for some damage limitation so life can go on somehow, neither Luke nor Carrie realizes they're holding their breath.

Vollie again: 'You muppet.'

'Go on, then – what are you waiting for?' Ben again, almost hysterical.

'I stuck my neck out for you. Family. That's what's important.'

'YOU FIND LOUIS. YOU ASK HIM ABOUT THAT BEEMER.'

'All right. Now can I go?'

A door slams downstairs. Luke and Carrie retreat to her room.

'How long's it been going on?' Luke says.

'Ages,' says Carrie. 'It started after tea.'

Another slam.

'Front door – Ben going out,' Carrie adds, checking her window. 'Let's hope Boyce doesn't come up.'

'Or Vollie . . . I know he's your brother, but –'

'He'll calm down in a minute. He isn't as bad as he seems. He rescued us, you know.'

'From?'

'Hermione Griffiths,' says Carrie. 'Ben was in Barnard Walsh –'

'The children's home.'

'We had to go into Care – care, that's a laugh. Ben got bullied and if it weren't for Si . . . After Mum died, Vollie applied for custody. He got us out one by one. I know he's a monster sometimes, but when he came up the drive that day –'

'Couldn't you live with Uncle Louis?'

'Too old to adopt or something. Obviously it was better for me to live in this crumbling old house with people who didn't love me. Sometimes I went to foster homes. You'd just get fond of the people and then you'd be moved somewhere else — and the *waiting*, and the not being told anything, having no power over your future or *anything that happens to you* —'

Luke hugs Carrie tightly. 'It's all right now,' he says.

Carrie dries her eyes. 'Vollie and Boyce came to get me. Had her long enough, have we? Vollie said. Boyce picked up the superintendent. Put him down, said Vollie. The superintendent never said anything. I promised Mum we'd stick together, Vollie said. They had to let me go after the forms were filled in — it was a Tuesday, that day.'

'Wasn't *that* bad, though, was it? Has to be better than this.'

'Easy for you to say,' Carrie says. 'What you don't understand is even a bad family *is better than no family at all*.'

Easy for him to say, with a stack of family Christmases behind him — Dad making sledges in the shed, Danny and Mum playing Twister, crackers, presents, circuses, grand-parents, holidays, accidents, family jokes, pets, nights in together, favourite films, camping trips, Mum's car — a million snapshots of past family life flash through Luke's mind in seconds. 'Maybe Si was his family.'

'Whose family?'

'Ben's,' Luke says.

'He tried to get Ben to go to college. Si wanted a different life for Ben.'

'Then the fire.'

'And the joyriding spiralling out of control . . . Si wanted them to get a place together. He was everything to Ben –'

'Think I get it,' Luke says. 'You all right now?'

'I'll survive.' Carrie shrugs. 'What will you do about the Beemer?'

'The what?'

'The BMW I'm assuming you didn't collect.'

'Solve that one when I come to it,' Luke says, the way he solves everything these days.

The night streets ring under Luke's feet as he takes the road home at two. Trekking between home and The Crock seems like his whole life lately. Danny telling him he'd stopped Wyndham leaving was the first time they'd talked in ages – and he, Luke, had shut him out. No surprise his brother's life is going on without him. Every time he comes home it's late at night and everyone's fast asleep. His own family seem like strangers sometimes, replaced by Carrie's family and their turbulent life at The Crock.

Exiting Gashouse Lane, Luke turns on to Breakwater Road.

A kid's sock in the road – Luke drapes it over a wall. Behind the wall looms the top of the Godzilla-sized Breakwater gasholder, dwarfing the smaller Albert across the street. Luke's feet drag slower and slower. What's to go home for? Wyndham's snoring? Time for an overview, why not?

The bottom of the razor-wired fence snags Luke's hoodie as he squeezes underneath it. The rusty ladder showers him with water, the gantries boom under his feet — then the dome. Kuh-bum, kuh-boom. The Albert sounds duller — fuller — than the last time he climbed it — when was it? — that night he and Danny had watched the Golf get nicked, the night of the opening of the locket —

The gasholder didn't have any gas in it, it didn't move up or down. Luke counts the rings of its frame, towering like a big top into the starry night sky above. Could be full of water or something — that'd make it sound different. And it did sound fuller somehow.

I could've put it on ice at the Albert, if you hadn't gone off your head. Vollie's sneering voice in the row at The Crock nags at the back of Luke's mind. Put *what* on ice in the Albert?

Too stirred up to enjoy the view, Luke slides back down the ladder with a foot either side of the rails. In the darkness pooling at the bottom of the gasholder, the outlines of a door roughly cut into its plating catch an edge of moonlight.

How come he never noticed it before? Luke feels around the door as far as he can reach and as low, his hand finding the ring of oily water in which the gasholder sits. Water drips somewhere inside it. Luke puts an ear to the plates. *Two drips now, one falling a long way on to concrete, the other not so far, on to metal.* The door in its side had been roughly cut through and across the metal plates by someone who didn't admire the gasholder or care about it at all. Luke tries to imagine someone doing it — where would they hide the key? *They ruined your gas-proof seal, Eden Fishlake. If you were me what would you do?*

An oily rock stares up at him like an eye in the

moonlight. Flipping it over, Luke discovers a pipe running along the side of the path. Following the pipe with his fingers, Luke's fingers find a crevice and, feeling around in it, a key! Fumbling the key into the padlock, Luke pushes open the door.

Wow! A dozen, forty, sixty motors, standing in rows in a dim dome with a light in the vault of its roof! As Luke's eyes adjust to the gloom, it's obvious that any light leaking in comes from gaps in the metal plates overlooking the Village, where the car park blazes all night. A channel filled with oil and water runs round the concrete floor. A regular drip plinks on to the roof of a dark-blue Corsair by the door.

Used-car heaven or what? *I could put it on ice in the Albert.* So Vollie's secret car lot gives up its secrets at last. Luke patrols the rows, picking out cars of choice, the faint niff of gas everywhere lending an air of James Bond-like excitement to the hidden Dome of Motors. *From his subterranean headquarters, evil genius Vollard Crocker schemes to take over the world . . .*

No accident, then, that Boyce Crocker got a job with Multiplex security. Handy for patrolling the Village car park outside their little investment. They could even drive stuff off and store it in here, and, though it was only metres away, no one would know where it was. Luke peers inside a Toyota Avensis. Not exactly your wish-list, but a discerning mix of executive faves, with the odd dash of class here and there, not a lot of rubbish, except that Citroën Xsara . . . *What's that?*

The screaming of metal on concrete announces the

closing of the double doors, their final slamming together bringing down a shower over Luke.

Luke ducks behind a Mondeo, his heart pounding in his chest with the ringing of the echoes overhead. After a while the steady plink-plink of the same old drip on the Corsair re-establishes itself. Luke rises cautiously and slips to the door, now padlocked. Omigod, he's locked in. They must've known someone was in here. *Probably they were keeping him on ice.*

A bit of casual snooping has closed on him like a trap. The once-dramatic HQ of Evil Vollard — *Come in, Mr Bond, I hope you like gas* — now seems like a scary place to have to spend the night. Tripping over a battery in the gloom, Luke scouts round the walls of the gasholder until he reaches the battery again. No more doors. No holes. No way out. Trapped like a pea in a drum. Good job it *isn't* gas-tight. A snooper could suffocate.

Luke sits in a Lotus Elise and tries to work out what to do.

Eden Fishlake or Ned or Bob wouldn't've panicked. They hadn't panicked when firebombs had rained on to the roof of the Vicky and the Albert. Luke looks up and a weak place in its armour winks over the first tier of plates. He rolls round an oil drum and stands on it, hits the weak place with a wrench. But the faint wink in the armour stays solid and out of reach . . .

Luke returns to the Lotus and wishes he could blast, Bond-like, through the walls of the Albert and shoot out over Marrowbone Slip to crash into the harbour, switch to an amphibious vehicle and drive off, laughing at Vollie. (Who was it who'd closed the doors? Any chance they'd think they'd swung open by themselves?) Eden Fishlake and Ned Beale hadn't stood around watching while the Albert exploded. *They'd climbed up and put it out and had saved the whole area in the process.* No point in waiting for Vollie to discover 'Cousin Louis' trapped in the gasholder, knowing a shedload of stuff he shouldn't. Better do something to save himself, but what?

He could ring Danny at home, but then there'd be a fuss.

Or he can tell it like it is. They've got no right to lock him in. He hasn't done anything wrong – ish. It takes guts to stand out from the crowd, but the Gashouse Lane Volunteers had done it. He'll be a hero if these motors are stolen, what's he – and everyone else – afraid of?

Luke fills his lungs and takes up his wrench.

He could keep quiet about it. He could take whatever's coming to Cousin Louis and stay under Boyce Crocker's thumb, like everyone else under the gasholders. He could lie to save himself, but what happened to a sense of community?

'Help! I'm stuck! Anyone!' Luke runs the wrench round the walls like a one-man steel band. He bangs on a Honda Civic. He bangs on a Citroën Xsara. He makes as much noise as he can. 'HELP! I'M IN THE WHITE HATS' CAR LOT! LOTS OF MOTORS WITH DODGY PLATES! ANYONE WITH THE BOTTLE TO COME AND LET ME OUT?'

8. Barnard Walsh

Next day, 'Want to go out to the Drome?' Ben offers, when he bumps into Luke in the street. 'Know where I can get hold of an Astra. Here, thirty quid — your share of the petrol take.'

'Keep it,' Luke says shortly.

'Vollie says, "Where's the Beemer?"'

'I left it where Boyce told me.'

'Where is it, then?'

'How do I know?'

'I need the keys now or I'm dog meat.'

'What d'you want me to do about it?' Luke says coldly.

'Don't like me, do you?' Ben says.

'You nicked my mum's car, or your mates did.'

'What d'you want me to do about it?'

'Just stick around,' Luke says. 'You'll get done for it sooner or later.'

'That's what Carmen says.'

'Get out before it's too late.'

'Carmen says that, as well. How come your mum's car was nicked around here? You live in Wales, don't you?'

'Brought me down here, didn't she?' Cousin Louis improvises, reminded somehow of Wyndham's mother's phone call. He'll ring her up and check it out one day soon, for a promise . . .

After a morning shift at Make It All, Luke fancies a film for a relaxing change from the drama of everyday life.

Waiting in line at the top of the staircase by the pick 'n' mix and ice-cream counter while Wyndham tears tickets for the two o'clock showing of Tracey Philips's latest action movie, wondering what kind of a name Tracey Philips is for a bloke anyway, Luke notes Wyndham's haircut. The borrowed socks. The official T tucked into the trousers – Danny's trousers, for a wonder. The goofy grin. The wanting-to-please film-buff conversation – Mind the steps, won't you? I like him too. Advent of Fear wasn't great, but I like the director . . . Did Cape Zenda too? Yeah, I know. You too. What a geek Wyndham is.

Finally Luke proffers his ticket. 'Hey, McNab.'

'Hey, Couch.' Wyndham peers at Luke's ticket. 'Bulletproof Vest – the Tracey Philips vehicle. Really?'

'Why not?'

'Better off in screen 5. Wending Ways is cool, plus the story's unusual –'

'About you staying with us,' Luke says, taking back his half-a-ticket.

'Or Countdown to Glory, screen 10, wicked effects. This tank goes into a train –'

'What went down here's better than that,' Luke

says. 'River of fire right through here when the gas-holders almost blew up. Right under where they built this place.'

Wyndham looks at him blankly. 'Screen 8, enjoy the film,' he says, tearing six more tickets and shepherding a group through the barriers.

'How long before they trace you?' Luke says, sorting out money for a Coke.

'Who?'

'The children's home. I know all about Barnard Walsh, I met someone else who went there. And don't bother giving me that guff about swapping bags on the train.'

Wyndham pales. 'Danny says I can stay.'

'Is that right?'

'You won't say anything, will you?'

'I won't, you will,' says Luke.

'I can't tell them now.'

'Why not?'

'Least I don't come from the monkey farm like you'. Wyndham looks at Luke. 'They don't call them children's homes any more. They call them temporary placements.'

'How did you find Auntie Marion?'

'Mrs Nettlefold – she works at Barnard Walsh. She's nice to me. She tells me stuff.' Wyndham tears three more tickets. 'Screen 7, enjoy the film. I got your number from her address book. I'd heard about your family. Thought I'd try it on. Usually works for two or three days if you get a mate to ring up and say you're staying the weekend. Then they come and find you.'

'Two or three days?' Luke says. 'You've been here about five *weeks*.'

'I've got a mate who covers for me. Bonnie's been out loads of times. It was her idea.'

'What's your real name?'

'Julian Coombes. I've wanted to be adopted since I was seven,' Wyndham says hollowly. 'I even put an ad in the paper: "Parents Wanted For Seven-Year-Old. Julian Is Intelligent and Caring." They told me I had initiative. But after I was nine, I knew it would never happen. They like to adopt little kids. Once you're nine, you're too old.'

'How old are you now?'

'Thirteen.'

'Won't you get into trouble?'

'I wanted a holiday,' Wyndham says. 'You live at Barnard Walsh.'

'What's it like, anyway?'

'Flat with these other boys.' Wyndham shrugs. 'Helen and David look after us, but when you're eighteen, you're out. They never even remembered Jamie's birthday. He couldn't get a job. Couldn't get a National Insurance number. He ended up on the street. He had a bit of shoplifting, nothing spectacular.'

'Didn't know Ben Crocker, did you?'

'Didn't know anyone long. First I was in Fielding-Knight, then two years in Talbot King, then Barnard Walsh. Before that it was Chaucer Nursery Unit, before that I had my mum. When I met Mrs Nettlefold she told me about the country. About how you moved from a village you lived in all your life. That's why I picked your number. I've never been to the beach. Or seen a cow or a horse.'

'You're having a laugh.'

'It's true.'

'So you just turned up,' Luke says.

'Mrs Nettlefold said you hadn't seen Wyndham since he was a baby. Seemed like a pretty good bet.'

'But your mum rang,' Luke says. 'I thought –'

'Bonnie,' Wyndham says. 'She's a mate. I do the same for her. They took me away from my mum. I haven't seen her since I was three.'

Luke's mind rewinds to Wyndham's arrival. 'So your dad's not a steeplejack.'

'I haven't got a dad.'

'That why you wanted mine – why you nicked his dad's pipe?'

'I never meant to keep it.'

'Cheers for that.'

'What will you do?' Wyndham says.

So Wyndham isn't what he seems. What is? The dimly lit cinema foyer is a palace of dreams, after all. Is it so bad to want a family, a dad, just for one summer holiday? *Even a bad family is better than no family at all.*

'Here's the deal,' Luke decides. 'I won't say anything yet because they must be closing in on you anyway, and the holidays're almost over, if you respect the parents and stay out of my face, all right?'

'Top banana,' says Wyndham incredulously. 'No one *ever* gives me a break –'

'Do me a favour, yeah? Never say "top banana" again.'

'Screen 5, enjoy the film. Where were you this morning anyway?' Wyndham says. 'I know you were out all night. I messed up your bed to cover for you.'

'Cheers,' Luke says. 'Mind your own. I told you, stay out of my face.'

'Did you climb the Albert again?'

'No. I got locked inside it.'

'Seriously?' Wyndham says.

'Hopefully whoever shut me in thinks he forgot to lock it. Anyway, it's out of the bag.'

'What is?'

'Everything,' Luke says. 'Old guy over the road heard me banging and had the guts to call the police. Now they've seized Vollie's motors.'

'What motors?'

'The Crockers store cars in the gasholder. Vollie'll be bricking it, even if they are legit, which most of them probably aren't.'

'What did you tell the cops?'

'Stuff,' Luke says. 'Not a lot.'

'Vollie knows PC Fox. You want to watch out.'

'How do you know?'

'Griffin Flashman,' says Wyndham. 'Jasper Flashman's brother? He works out at Muscles Gym. He knows a lot about Vollie.'

'Let him watch out,' Luke says. 'I don't care what Vollie does. The old bloke over the road's had his house done over twice but he still had the bottle to call the police and say he saw stuff going down, cars in and out of the Albert. They're bullies,' Luke says, 'not serious crims. If everyone stops being afraid of the Crockers we can fight back, like the Gashouse Lane Volunteers.'

'The who?'

'Never mind,' says Luke. 'I'm starting the New Volunteers – posse against the White Hats. Interested?'

'Like the Guardians in New York? Riding the tube and protecting people, that kind of thing?'

'Kind of, yeah,' Luke says.

Wyndham considers. 'Is there a uniform with that?'

'Whatever you want.'

'OK, Chief.'

Luke walks the lonely plush corridor towards *Bulletproof Vest* on screen 9. 'Oh, and McNab?'

'Chief?'

'Hands off the Turk's head, all right?'

It all turns pear-shaped that evening. First a police car pulls away from The Crock as Luke turns into the Ope. Then, entering The Crock silently, 'Louis' overhears Boyce: 'HOW DO I KNOW WHY?'

Vollie: 'Your man bell you or what?'

'KEYS TURNED UP IN THE POST.'

'What's going on?' Ben's voice.

'LOUIS LEFT THE BEEMER ON ROYAL PARADE –'

'Actually I thought it was safer on the main drag,' Cousin Louis bluffs, entering boldly. 'And you want to check the door on the Albert. Noticed it swinging last night.'

Vollie draws out a kitchen chair. 'Louis, take the weight off your feet.' He pours from a pot of tea. 'I'll be Daddy, shall I?'

Luke takes a cuppa, heart pounding.

Vollie watches Luke's chin as he drinks. 'Heard what went down last night?'

'I was out on a job, remember?'

'Meet your man, then, did you?'

'Too much heat at the lay-by. Got him to tail me to Royal Parade and mail the keys to me after.' Sweat trickles down Luke's sides inside his clothes as he hears himself inventing dialogue from *The Bill*. 'So what went down last night?'

'Big man's on duty at the Village,' Vollie says, meaning Boyce, 'when he hears someone up on the Albert —'

'DOOR'S OPEN WHEN I GET ROUND THERE.'

'Forget to lock up, did you?' Vollie sneers.

'GOT A LOT ON MY MIND.'

'We keep a few motors in the Albert. Not many people know that.' Vollie watches Louis. 'Benny-boy mention it, did he?'

'First thing I told him,' Ben covers. 'I thought he should know everything.'

Luke looks at him gratefully.

'Boyce locks up,' Vollie continues. 'Time I get round there, police're all over the car yard like a rash — You look like you're going to puke.'

'Just wondering what we've got in there,' Cousin Louis says faintly.

'Police impound the lot and now I've got to account for 'em, thanks to some Nose making a call –'

'That pimple Jasper Flashman,' Ben says.

'Louis – any ideas?'

'How would I know?'

'Thought you might –'

'– GIVE US A CLUE. TOP-UP?' Boyce says, wielding the teapot over Cousin Louis's sweating head.

The door slams and Carrie comes in. 'I got a new job, guess what?'

Jeeves comes out from under the table and sniffs Carrie's shoes. Boyce puts down the teapot. No one says anything.

'Helping out at the college,' Carrie answers her own question brightly. 'I'm temping in student admissions from Monday the 8th for six weeks.'

'La-de-da,' says Vollie.

'Now I can pay for driving lessons.'

'I'M TEACHING YOU, AREN'T I?'

'Thanks, Boyce, but I –'

'I'M TEACHING YOU,' Boyce says, fetching a mugful of pencils and snapping out a knife to sharpen them.

Carrie shrugs off her jacket and cuts up a bowl of fruit. She glances at Luke. 'All right, Louis?'

Vollie snarls, 'Why'd you eat monkey food?' and goes out in the yard to polish his gnomes and throw a steak to Jeeves before vaulting the wall to a pub called the Punch Bowl and drinking all night with people terrified of him.

'Those gnomes in the yard,' Luke says. 'There's one by the front door as well.'

'What about them?' Carrie says, slicing an apple briskly.

'He always collect gnomes?'

'No *always*, is there?' Carrie shrugs.

'Round my house there is,' Luke says after a moment.

Carrie looks at him warningly.

'Gnomes are the least of your worries, mate.' Boyce reaches for another pencil. Luke looks at him. There's nothing in Boyce's manner to indicate that he might have glimpsed 'Cousin Louis' in the darkness of the gasholder when he closed the double doors – and nothing to indicate that he hasn't. 'Least of your worries,' Boyce says again, not speaking in capitals for once. Producing a nice point with measured strokes of his knife and admiring it before selecting another pencil, his eyes meet Luke's over the table.

As Luke gets up to escape, there's a knock at the door.

Boyce snaps up his knife. 'I GOT IT.'

Light floods down the hall from the open front door. To one side of Boyce's lumbering outline an apparition appears on the step – Wyndham, in an extraordinary red 'uniform' of pullover, dyed army-surplus hat and extravagant chains of office. 'Is Luke there?'

'WHO?'

'My cousin Luke, I followed him here – Yo, Luke!' Wyndham waves down the corridor. 'Your mum says, "Can you come home?"'

Boyce looks round with the Wrath of Khan. 'LOUIS? SOMEONE TO SEE YOU.'

9. Straight

I don't feel real since Luke read my diary — 'True Confessions', I'm calling them, but I may stop writing them now. Ben's been quiet lately, but I'm not holding my breath. They got over the Audi, and Luke smoothed the Beemer somehow. Now Vollie's going mad over the car yard, turning over the happy home for account books he left somewhere. It feels stupid to write about it. I can't help Ben anyway. All I can do is help myself. The new job's a start.

Luke says, 'Keep Confessing.' He reckons writing it all down'll help me to see how I feel. Trouble is, I don't feel anything. I feel like a fly stuck in jelly — not going up or down or anywhere fast. I feel like my life's on hold.

Luke says I'm never straight with him, but that's not true — I try to be as straight as I can. It's not easy to say, 'My mum died,' or, 'My brothers've got a chip on their shoulder. They tend to lash out because that's all they know how to do.'

Vollie, Boyce, Ben — Jasper Flashman at Make It All, Miranda, my mate from school — they're all more solid than I am. I don't feel crooked, I don't feel straight — I feel like someone's shadow.

Shadow-Carrie didn't ask to be rescued. She got used to blending into the background. She didn't ask to have a real live Luke Couch skating into her life.

I can't fry eggs forever. What am I, Lorna Doone? Soon as I pass my driving test I'm out of here and driving into the sunset to some place no one ever heard the name 'Crocker'.

Then I'll be straight with Luke, straight with myself, forever.

— Confessions of Carmen Crocker

'You've come on by leaps and bounds,' smiles Diana Buchanan. 'Have you been practising, Luke?'

As getaway car for the White Hats. 'Just a bit,' Luke says.

'And this is your — sixth lesson?'

'Seventh.'

'So it's hill starts today — again . . . ' Diana Buchanan notes on her schedule. 'And Julie says, "Can you ring her?"'

Juliet Buchanan. *Will* she take a hint? Luke straps in and engages first gear after the usual gurning into his mirrors. 'So how long before I pass?' he says.

'Theory test first.'

'Do what?'

Diana Buchanan hands Luke a form. 'Fill this in. Turn up when they tell you. Learn your Highway Code.'

After a number of rattling hill starts on testing slopes around town, Luke requests a burn on the Parkway. Diana Buchanan takes him out via the Blue Monkey interchange, which has Luke well confused. After a shaky start, he practises three-point turns in the Blue Monkey Industrial Estate, then reverse-parks neatly around a corner. 'Good, aren't I?' Luke says. 'So when can I take my test?'

'Now, if you want to fail it. Pull away when you're ready.'

'How many more lessons, d'you think? Mum says she might –'

'*Stop!*' Diana Buchanan raps the dash with her biro.

Luke stands on the brake and clutch, bringing the 206 to a halt in a straight line.

'Nice emergency stop. I think we can tick that one off.'

Luke goes to neutral and handbrake and watches it ticked off the list.

'And what would you do now, if the examiner doesn't ask you to do anything?'

'Start the car, mirrors, signal, manoeuvre – pull into a safe position?'

Diana Buchanan's biro moves down her list. 'Speed limit on a motorway?'

'Seventy miles an hour.'

'Speed limit on the Parkway?'

'Dual carriageway's same speed limit as a motorway, 'cept lorries can use the fast lane.'

'And what *didn't* you do on the slip road?'

'Blend with the speed of the traffic?'

Diana Buchanan puts away her clipboard. 'Pull away in your own time.'

Luke pulls away through a sweet change from first to second. 'So when d'you think I'll be ready?'

'Your worst problem's overconfidence,' Diana Buchanan says drily, 'but you've made a lot of progress. I should think the 23rd.'

'Next month – *for real?*'

'We'll put you in for your test. No guarantees, of course. You'll need at least six more lessons –'

'Sign me up,' Luke says. 'It's a deal.'

Everything about the morning, from Diana Buchanan's cat brooch winking on her lapel to the road unwinding in front of him, seems to hold, at last, the promise of being able to *drive*.

'Brake,' says Diana Buchanan. 'Who *is* that in the middle of the road?'

''S'only Danny,' says Luke, ignoring Danny's Vees and pulling in beside him. 'Want a lift, you spod? We're going home.'

'No-brainer asks schoolboy for help finding his own house,' says Danny, introducing his new rucksack into the back seat in a bag reading 'Back to School'.

'Have we met?' says Diana Buchanan.

'A rare glimpse of the shy Lesser-Sighted Danbo Destructor-Bird leaving its habitat. He hibernates when he's not eating sugar. He's only my brother,' Luke says.

'Jules?' Luke rings Diana Buchanan's daughter later from the corner near the ice rink. 'The thing is, I've been away. Yeah. And now I'll be going to college, and I'm going to be really busy . . . Me and Carrie made up, yeah. We're not going out or anything . . . That day at the aquarium? I was *going* to . . . Jules? Hullo?'

So having a driving lesson with her mum had reminded him that finishing with Juliet Buchanan wasn't going to be easy. When had they *started*, he'd like to know.

Pocketing his mobile, Luke bumps into a flushed-looking Carrie under the fake snow by the ticket office. The Swiss Cottage Ice Rink shares the Millennium Buildings with a swimming pool and a basketball court.

'How'd the driving lesson go?' Carrie asks.

'Magic,' says Luke. 'No problem. Putting me in for my test.'

'Wow. Can you teach me?'

'Thought Boyce was teaching you.'

'Would you like Boyce to teach you?' Carrie buys tickets and hands Luke a token for skate hire. 'See you on the ice — You can skate, can't you?'

Luke takes the token. 'Course.'

Looking out for Carrie on the ice after a nasty struggle with a pair of hard leather skating boots, Luke spots her at last doing a twirl. She looks so cute flying round the rink, waving for him to join her, that the Swiss Cottage, with its half-timbered walls, cheesy lights and disco music, seems like some land out of time where everyone's red-cheeked and happy. How hard can skating be?

Luke steps out on to the ice; manages three tottering steps; lunges for the barrier. Setting out again — it isn't as easy as it looks — he trips, stumbles and windmills his way round the rink before crashing spectacularly in the middle and nutting the ice.

'Can't skate, can you?' Carrie appears like a fairy, her blades cutting a shower of snow. 'Want any help?'

'I'm good.'

Luke gets up and sets off again, his ankles feeling like

jelly. Carrie's hand creeps into his. They wobble round together until a boy in a white hat cuts between them. Two others appear on either side, throwing shapes as they power round the inside track, scattering small children in front of them.

'Ice-hogs!' Luke shouts after them, windmilling backwards to save himself.

One of them circles back to chat with Carrie.

'Mates of Ben's,' Carrie says, rejoining Luke. 'Someone they know says they saw *Simon Bradshaw* back from the dead.'

'Who?'

'Ben's mate Simon? It's only a stupid rumour.'

'They *saw* him?' Luke says. 'Where?'

'Sitting in a Fiesta at some traffic lights. He looked across and drove off. It must've been someone else. Come on, let's forget it. Haven't you ever been skating before?' Carrie adds, helping Luke up.

'Ages ago,' Luke says. 'Bus to Tarmouth only came once a week.'

'Once a *week*,' Carrie laughs. 'Country life, eh?'

'I miss it,' Luke says, wobbling off.

Afterwards, in the Edelweiss Café, Luke necks a plate of chips. 'Thing is,' he tells Carrie, 'I can't come round any more. It's freaking me out that they suspect.'

'Your cousin turning up on the doorstep, you mean?'

'He isn't my cousin,' Luke says. 'He's this kid from Barnard Walsh who landed on us for a holiday.'

'How did you get rid of him in front of Boyce?' Carrie says. 'Without inviting him in?'

'Said he was some weirdo who had me down as someone else.'

'Did Boyce go for it?'

'Wyndham looks like an idiot in that stupid uniform he's making. Boyce shut the door on him. But they're watching me all the time.'

'It doesn't matter,' says Carrie. 'They can't know anything for sure unless they contact the real Louis and he was going away on a round-the-world trip. That's why he didn't think he'd make it when Vollie asked.'

'I dunno,' Luke says. 'Vollie looks at me sometimes. Maybe he remembers me from Make It All.'

'He's just mad cos they seized his motors and he's got to prove they're his. Ben slams in and out of the house. He could do anything –'

'Don't worry about it,' says Luke. 'Would the New Volunteers desert you?'

'Who?'

'The Red Hats – New Volunteers. Action posse against street aggro. Wyndham's doing this uniform. Did you *see* what he was wearing?'

'N-oo,' says Carrie. 'What?'

'Luke!' A girl with a dark wing of hair over her face pauses with a tray and a pushchair.

'Liv.' Luke flushes. 'No way.'

'Anyone sitting here?'

'Help yourself.'

'This is Kieran Mark. He's three now.'

'No way.'

Luke helps the baby's legs into an Edelweiss Café high chair. The chubby little boy regards Luke seriously as he dips a chip in ketchup.

'It's fine,' the girl says.

Luke advances the chip. Kieran Mark transfers it to his mouth without taking his eyes off Luke.

Carrie clears her throat.

'Carrie,' Luke says, 'Liv.'

'Been skating?'

'I have,' Carrie says. 'He hasn't.'

'I've been arsing,' says Luke.

'I used to live next door to Luke when he did a carwash,' Liv says.

The neighbour who got pregnant. Carrie looks at her.

'Like your chips, don't you?' Luke says, tantalizing Kieran Mark. 'Want some more ketchup on that?'

'He's a lovely boy,' says Carrie.

'And Kieran,' Liv jokes.

'His hair's grown loads,' Luke says. 'You want some gel on that, mate.'

'What are you doing now?' Liv says.

'Starting college in September.'

'Doing?'

'GNVQ in Leisure and Tourism.'

'That what you want to do?'

'It is, yeah, why not?' Suddenly Luke feels that it *is* what he wants to do.

Carrie watches them connecting over the bubble of the recent past, where no one else exists. Liv fishes a chip from the trough in Kieran's plastic bib. Still the connection isn't broken. 'I always thought you'd do a people thing.'

'This *is* a people thing.'

'GNVQs don't qualify you for much.'

'It's a start, isn't it?' Luke says. 'It'll lead into other things.' Suddenly he feels that it will.

'How's Danny?' Liv wonders.

'Don't see much of him these days. What about you?'

'I'm at uni now. Kieran's at home with Mum.'

'Where?' Luke asks.

'Oxmouth,' Liv says, naming the next big town. 'The city's great. I'm starting a new life. It's hard looking after yourself, but you get to make your own choices –'

'I'd kill to get away and start my own life,' Carrie says evenly.

Luke looks at her.

'I've got to get away from them *now* – can't you under-stand? I can't wait.'

'Hey,' says Luke. 'It's all right.'

'You don't know how lucky you are,' Carrie says to Liv. Tears spill over and run down her face unconsciously. 'I'd do anything to get out of here.'

'Hey,' Luke says again. 'She's all right,' he says to Liv. 'She hurt her leg on the ice.'

'We'd better go,' Liv says.

'You don't have to do that,' says Carrie.

'We're late for the bus anyway. Luke – it's all right –'

'I've got him. You do good for Mummy,' Luke tells Kieran Mark, strapping him into his pushchair.

'I'm sorry,' says Carrie. 'I didn't mean –'

'I've got a spare bed in hall. You should come up. It's a lot of fun. I can show you round uni any time if you're thinking of applying.' Liv scribbles a number on a serviette and hands it to Carrie. 'Give me a ring. Any time.'

'I couldn't.'

'Any friend of Luke's.'

Carrie meets Liv's frank brown eyes and folds away the serviette. *Thank you*, her eyes say to Liv's.

Luke turns out his lower lip, smacks himself on the back of the head and pops the lip in again. The clouds pass from Kieran Mark's face and he brings out a toothy smile.

'Good to see you're still loony,' says Liv.

'Always,' says Luke. 'Take care.'

'Bye-bye, baby.' Carrie waves Kieran Mark to the door. The little boy waves back by opening and closing his fist. 'He's so cute,' Carrie says.

'She must be feeding him Baby Bio or something – he never had that much hair.' Luke looks at her. 'All right now?'

'Sorry about that. I'm unhappy at home, but –' Carrie sighs. 'I don't know *what* I feel any more.'

'Don't worry about it,' Luke says.

Carrie watches the double doors close on the pushchair. 'What is it with you and her?'

What is it, but knowing each other a long time? There's more to it than that. Liv's searching brown eyes asking him, does he *want* to do a GNVQ? Laughingly backing off when she sees that yes, he does – that everything's right with him, knowing him as well as she does, like no one else will, somehow. 'We lived next door to each other for ages – then I bought this toy for Kieran Mark and her boyf crashed his motor, good job, he was scum. Liv 'n' I are mates, what d'you think?' Luke says. 'No, Kieran Mark isn't like me.'

'You were good with him.'

'Think I've finally grown up. You've got a chip on your shoulder,' Luke adds.

Carrie looks round.

'Gotcha,' Luke grins.

'You're such a big kid,' Carrie says.

'By the way,' Luke says to his mother a couple of days later, 'Bowden's parents are going away and he's asked me to stay a few days.'

'Michael from snooker club again? Where are they going?'

'Somewhere beginning with B.'

'Barcelona? Balearics?'

Luke looks at his mother. 'Barbados,' he lies to her face. 'I'm looking after his goldfish called Brillo, so I might be coming and going.'

'But won't he be there?'

'He works odd hours.'

'Well, as long as you check in sometimes.'

So far, so good. Luke leaves the room as casually as he appeared to saunter into it. Covered for a few days at one end, at least. His absences at the Crocker end aren't going to be so easily accounted for, but the whole double-life nightmare's just about covered, although hanging by a thread – until Wyndham starts up at dinner.

'There's a new one,' Wyndham announces, position- ing the red hat he's been wearing lately neatly beside his plate.

'A new what?' says Danny. 'How come the PlayStation's always in your room these days?'

'Haven't *seen* you for ages, that's why,' Wyndham says. 'Stop hanging out at the gym with Griffin Flashman.'

'Not *me* who's hanging out with Griffin Flashman.'

'He's helping me with posters for the Red Hats, all right?' Wyndham says defensively.

'The Red Hats,' Dad says. 'I've heard about them. They help people cross the road.'

Danny looks at him.

'As-I-was-saying, there's a new Crocker.' Wyndham helps himself to shepherd's pie. 'There's a cousin called Louis now – I saw him with Boyce going into their house – *and* out with Vollard, counting their stolen cars. Shepherd's pie, Luke?' Wyndham holds out the spoon insinuatingly.

'Vollie,' says Luke. 'Not Vollard.'

'You'd know,' Wyndham says.

Luke looks daggers back at him. '*Julian's* a nice name, isn't it?' he says, taking the spoon off Wyndham. 'Julian Coombes, heard it on the news or something –'

'Wyndham, are you all right?' Mum says. 'Danny, slip out and get Wyndham a drink –'

'I'm all right,' Wyndham chokes.

'Give him a pat on the back.'

Luke slaps Wyndham hard three times in the middle of his back.

'Thanks, Louis,' says Wyndham, with venom.

'My pleasure, Coombes,' says Luke.

'The new insurance man called,' Mum says. 'He's young, very nice —'

'He came in and played *Ghostriders*,' says Danny. 'He almost beat me, but then he didn't.'

'Anyway, the cheque's coming through. What kind of car d'you fancy, Luke?'

'Talking of names, my father's name was Clement,' Dad says. 'Clement Attlee Couch. Funny sort of idea.'

'TVR or a Ferrari,' Luke says.

'Realistically?'

'VW or an Impreza.'

'Realistically?'

'Fiesta or a 306?'

'Signed on a 306 yesterday.'

Luke drops his fork. 'No way.'

'Pass your test and we'll share it,' Mum says. 'No kidding, kiddo.'

'That's not fair!' Danny shouts. 'He gets half a car and I get to move in with Wyndham!'

'Only while I'm rollering your room,' Mum says. 'Like the colour, don't you?'

'I don't *want* my room repainted. Wyndham threw up in his —'

'You won't try the pipe again, will you, Wyndham?'

'Not after last time,' Wyndham says. 'It just about made me sick.'

'Makes *me* sick I'm in with him.'

'Danny.'

'Well,' Danny says, 'his floor stinks.'

'Where's my holdall gone?' Wyndham shoots at Luke.

His mother looks at Luke. 'I thought there was something going on. Did you take Wyndham's things?'

'Yeah,' Luke says. 'I took them to *Barnard Walsh's* house and left them there by mistake.'

'Well, we'll have to get them back. Where does he live?'

'It's only a couple of jumpers,' Wyndham back-pedals.

'You must want your holdall back.'

'It's fine, Auntie Cath. Lovely tea. That's actually my coat you're wearing?' he says to Luke.

Mum rescues the coat from the back of Luke's chair. 'This is Barnard Walsh's. We'd better go and sort it out. How on earth have you got muddled up?'

Wyndham gets up abruptly and straightens his dyed red hat. 'I'm going out to meet Flashman.'

'Jasper Flashman?' says Dad.

'Me and Griffin meet him after work. Can't be too careful,' says Wyndham. Saluting oddly, he leaves the room.

'Funny outfit,' Dad says. 'You wonder what goes through his mind.'

'Nice one,' Luke goes, intercepting Wyndham in the hall. 'Coming round The Crock and almost getting me *killed* the other day.'

'I thought we were going to do something about that git who pushed me in the face,' Wyndham whispers back fiercely. 'I trusted you – and you're one of them.'

'I'm working undercover, you idiot.'

'What for?'

'To rescue my girlfriend.'

'Maybe she doesn't need rescuing. Maybe you like being a Crocker. I found a white hat in your room.'

'You don't understand,' says Luke. 'Ever heard of a mole –'

'A rat, more like. And you've got a family who think you're straight with them.'

Curling his lip, Guardian of the Streets 'Wyndham Nettlefold' slams out of the house and marches importantly down the steps, but not before Danny's wodge of wet loo paper dropped from their shared bedroom window hits Guardian Nettlefold's hat squarely in the centre . . .

At Standish Ope all that week, account books litter the floor. Vollie chases car purchases through some of them and invents car purchases in others. Boyce growls around the house. The phone rings at odd times. Spreadsheets showing sales figures are constantly up on the computer. Ben's supposed to tie them in with the motors. 'Louis' ducks out when he can. He knows Boyce is watching him.

'They should've kept proper accounts,' Carrie worries. 'We might even go out of business.'

'*We?*' Luke looks at her. How much does Carrie know? 'What about the people whose cars Vollie's nicked?'

'Ben stole cars, not Vollie. He's having counselling for it.'

'*Counselling?*' Luke says.

'He only got done for it once.'

'Come round to mine for tea. You haven't been over for ages.'

'Not till you teach me to drive,' Carrie counters.

'Can't, can I?' Luke says. 'You've got to be twenty-one and a qualified driver.'

'You could teach me off-road.'

'Where?'

'Multiplex car park, at night?'

'Boyce,' Luke reminds her.

'Seriously. I have to learn. It's my only way out of here.'

'We could go out to the Drome.'

'Who with?'

'The new insurance bloke's cool. He came over the other day with Mum's cheque and let me drive his Fiesta. He might come out with us.'

'What, in your mum's new car?'

'It'll be half mine as well.'

'I'll have half a teatime at yours, then, shall I?' Carrie pulls on a white hat. 'By the way, your "cousin" is called Julian Coombes. I recognize him from the Walsh.'

'I know,' Luke says. 'Don't blow him out when you come over, will you?'

'Thought we were being straight.'

'There's straight and there's proper,' says Luke.

10. River of Fire

The river of fire bursts out of the side of the gasholder, scorching a path through the gasworks, bursting into the huts where the workers soap their chests, their shirts hanging on pegs puffing one by one into flames as it passes. Like a livid orange snake the river rushes on, questing through alleyways, igniting doors and whole buildings, spilling down the aisle in the cinema, through the cinema stalls, where people scream and hold up their feet and popcorn spills everywhere. It rushes on to China Slip, to join the fire at the casino, where Ben spins a roulette wheel and rakes towards him model cars and a box of white hats and gnomes –

Bringgg – bringgg!

Luke sits up in bed with a mouth like the bottom of a birdcage. Alone in the house on his day off, the doorbell *would* have to ring.

'Aw'right!' Luke grumbles, thumping downstairs. Rubbing his eyes, he opens the door. 'Yes?'

'Julian Coombes?' says the man on the step.

'He's not in,' Luke says, wishing he'd said, 'Who?'

'Social Services.' The man flashes identification. 'Perhaps we could call back later.'

'Mum's in at six.'

'This would be him?' The man flashes a photo of Wyndham. 'Can I ask what he's doing here?'

'Having a holiday,' Luke says. 'I'm burning my breakfast. Sorry.'

Closing the door firmly on Social Services, Luke does actually burn his breakfast. Leaving the scorched frying pan to heal itself, he reads a note on the table saying, 'Gone to zoo with Danny and Wyndham, Mum x', and watches daytime telly in a comatose state before finally showering and dressing and going out.

Turning on to Commercial Road, he tries to ignore Ben Crocker, who crosses the street to join him. 'Coming fishing?'

'No.'

Ben shows him a stick with a hook. 'Know what this is for?'

'I'm guessing it's something illegal.'

'You're a fake,' Ben accuses.

'What d'you mean?' Luke says.

'Thought you knew something about the motor trade. Vollie won't like it when he finds out you made a fool of him.'

'Meaning?'

'Come fishing,' Ben says again. 'Everyone thinks I'm a car thief. Might as well act like one.'

'Why would I come with you?'

'I'll tell Vollie who you are if you don't.'

'Do what?'

'Carrie and I look out for each other,' Ben says, meeting Luke's eyes. 'I make a point of knowing who she hangs out with.'

'Fishing' takes up the rest of the afternoon and proves to be pretty high-risk, even for the lookout on the corner, who whistles once or twice coincidentally when neighbours peer out or walk by. As Ben pokes a stick through their letter boxes and angles meanly for their car keys, the residents of Boxtrees Estate are peacefully out in their gardens or turning the pages of their newspaper, the cars outside on their drives announcing that their car keys are up for grabs, on a table or a hook in the hall.

'Sometimes they don't lock the door,' Ben says. 'Saturday mornings is good, when they're doing odd jobs round the house. You can snatch the keys and drive away, no problem.'

'Can we go now?' Luke says.

'Stop stressing. You're only on lookout. Gonna try for that Shogun over there.'

'Curtains twitching,' Luke warns from inside the collar of his jacket.

Ben checks the house opposite. 'Forget it,' he decides, as a figure looms behind the window. 'Split up on the next street, all right?'

Producing a second bamboo from the side of his

combats, Ben twists in a hook and hands it to Luke. 'Meet up on Stoneport Road with any scores, all right?'

'Scores?'

'Keys, you dope. Millennium Buildings car park at nine?'

'Whatever.'

'Some quality stuff on Myerson Drive, yeah, but watch your back –'

'Thought you weren't going to do this any more.'

'Can't change what you are, can you?' Ben shrugs and walks away.

Luke watches Ben turn the corner like the Artful Dodger scouting for mild-mannered gentlemen with fob watches hanging off their waistcoats. Heading out of Boxtrees Estate on his way to the snooker hall, Luke flips his 'fishing rod' into a hedge.

Coming out on the Riverpark roundabout, the back of Make It All looms with some ruck going on behind it.

Luke turns into the shadowy street with the six o'clock sun behind him to find Jasper Flashman locking up with Vollard Crocker breathing down his neck and Wyndham in his New Volunteers 'uniform' jumping up and down between them.

'Going to hand over the keys, then, are we?' Vollie sneers.

'In a million years,' Jasper says.

'SOON AS.' Boyce looms out of the shadows.

'I know self-defence, I do.' Wyndham jumps up and down.

'Fancy a patio set, don't we?'

'THAT'S RIGHT.'

'You haven't got a hope in hell of getting it here,' Jasper Flashman says bravely. 'I'm not handing over the keys to you, so you might as well do what you like.'

'We've got rights, we have,' says Wyndham.

'Tell it to PC Fox,' Vollie sneers. 'Your old man been cheating the betting shop lately, Flashman?'

'Leave my dad out of it,' Jasper says, white with anger.

'I c'n ask him something for you, 'f you want me to take a message,' Luke says, sauntering down the street. 'Want me to ask him to keep anything for you?'

Flashman turns. Luke Couch stands outlined against the evening sky. Slowly he raises his hand.

Flashman draws back his arm and sends the bunched keys of Make It All in a long arc down the street, the evening sun winking on the keys to the safe as they fall into Luke's outstretched hand.

'Louis,' says Vollie. 'Nice timing.'

'HAND THEM OVER, COZ.'

As the evening sun throws their shadows at his feet, Wyndham and Jasper and Vollie and Boyce look down the street towards Luke. Vollie extends his hand and begins a slow walk towards him: 'Don't want to keep the bank manager waiting, do we? Nice little deposit in there waiting for us to bank it. How about it, Louis?'

The keys burn cold in Luke's grasp. Scenarios race through his brain, pulling him this way, then the other —

Greavesie finding the Make It All safe empty next morning; Vollie and Boyce in custody with their gnomes, Wyndham's shining face as they're arrested; his own windows kicked in, if they are. In the moments before he makes up his mind to blow his cover forever and earn the unending revenge of the Crockers, a million different images tumble through 'Louis's' brain –

Vollie's fingers curl. 'C'mon, you bogey-flick, what are we waiting for?'

Wyndham dances behind him. 'To me, Luke! To me!'

Thanks for nothing, McNab. Slowly Luke raises his arm.

'Jaz! What's up?' Griffin Flashman, Jasper's brother, turns the corner. Impressive pecs bulge from his sleeveless T. He looks as though he's hewn out of leather.

'Griff!' Jasper nods to Luke.

Luke bowls Griffin the keys. Vollie hisses and turns like a snake. Griffin tucks the keys into his pocket.

'Is there a problem?' he says to Vollie.

'My brother,' says Jasper. 'He's a bodybuilder.'

Boyce produces a snooker cue from behind his back and taps it on his palm. 'THINK YOU GOT SOMETHING OF OURS.'

'Nah,' Griff says. 'I don't think so.' Taking a red hat like Wyndham's from his back pocket, he slowly smooths it on, showing the depth of his arms and chest. 'Pity they're redeveloping here. I always thought this area would make a nice park for the kids.'

'NICE PARK,' Boyce repeats.

'Leave it, will you?' Vollie brings out a dog's lead,

whistling up a non-existent Jeeves to cover his retreat down the street.

Jasper gives him the finger. 'Go on,' he jeers. 'Get out!'

'Showing yourself up for what you really are?'

'That's what *you're* doing,' shouts Wyndham.

'We know all about you, Flashman,' Vollie shouts back.

'You're not even a proper villain, you're just a pathetic loser,' says Jasper.

'I'd like to shove this snooker cue *right* –'

Wyndham darts after Vollie. 'You can get arrested for that!'

Vollie picks him up by his collar, where a Barnard Walsh name-tag looks at him – and drops him again without a word.

Turning with sun behind him, Vollie sneers at them all – at Make It All, Griff, the world, the father who never valued him and then abandoned him, and ran off. 'You've *had it*, Flashman.' Raining a hail of blows weighted with broken promises, hurt feelings, clipped ears and lonely nights sobbing alone, Vollie kicks in the side of a car parked at the end of the street. '*You're history, you morons. It's personal!*'

Luke watches, horrified. When will he stop?

Vollie wipes his mouth. Turning to Luke as though nothing's happened, 'Coming, Louis?' he says. 'I'd like a word.'

'Have to be stupid, wouldn't I?'

'Work something out, can't we?' spits Vollie, turning on Luke his twisted face, unable for once to conceal himself or the kind of 'word' they'd have.

Coming, Louis?

Luke takes a moment to find his answer deep inside himself.

'NO! MY NAME'S NOT LOUIS AND I'M *NEVER COMING WITH YOU AGAIN!*'

That evening after basketball Luke spots a commotion in the road. 'Car chase on Union Junction!'

'Where?' Carrie says, pressing her head to the side of the stinky perspex tunnel between the Millennium Buildings and its multi-storey car park.

Beneath them a Vectra jumps the lights on the roundabout, its back end smoking and sliding away, before roaring off down the street. A police car wails after it. Moments later the squeal of tyres up the spiral ramps of the multi-storey car park echoes into the perspex tunnel.

Carrie looks at Luke. He reads in her face that it's Ben. 'He's coming into the car park!'

Meet me at Millennium Buildings car park when you score. Luke drops his basketball programme and races down the urine-smelling tunnel. He flings back the door on level 3 as the Vectra squeals up the ramp.

Windmilling into its path, Luke glimpses Ben at the wheel. As the Vectra slews sideways, Ben dives to open the passenger door. 'Get in!'

'No!'

'I'll hit you! *Get in now!*'

Overtaking and cranking the wheel over hard, Ben tries to avoid a pillar. In slow motion the open door yawns in front of Luke. As the only way to dodge it, Luke dives for the passenger seat.

Ben floors the accelerator and hits the ramp to level 4. On level 4 he parks like a shot and kills the engine dead. Missing the trail of exhaust, the police car squeals up to level 5. Ben gets up and floors it all the way down to Exit and away on Royal Parade and out to Riverpark by Mudd Mills and beyond it on to the Parkway.

'What did you open the door for?' Luke shouts.

'Don't say you're not enjoying it!' Ben turns to grin at him and give the finger to life.

On the moor road a second police car appears, turning up its siren and weaving behind them on to the Moor View roundabout. Ben goes off-road beyond it over a golf course and through a field of sheep, opening up down a straight forestry track between gloomy rows of black conifers. At the end of the former railway the mouth of a tunnel waits.

'Still coming,' Luke says, looking behind.

'Hang on!'

Increasing his speed, Ben throws the car through the old railway tunnel and instantly darkness falls, a blackness so thick and intense that Luke screams for 'Lights!'

'No time!'

Ben keeps straight on and they burst out at last on to the Drome, where a third police car waits.

'Damn!'

Ben throws the wheel round again and careers back through a stone quarry and the Blue Monkey Industrial Estate as a helicopter swings overhead.

'Chopper! We've had it — unless —'

Driving over a field and crashing on to the Leyton Way dual carriageway, Ben drives up the central reservation and under the gasworks railway tunnel to find the gasholders towering over him. Squealing right on to Gashouse Lane, left at the lights, he skids on the wet ground of Marrowbone Slip and as Luke covers his eyes the last thing he sees, as they slew sideways towards it, is the sign on the side of the aquarium saying BEHIND THIS WALL IS THE DEEPEST TANK IN EUROPE!

11. Brad

Hiding out at the Drome isn't easy. Police cars patrol its limits and monitor recent car wrecks. Still, the secret nuclear bunker under airstrip 3 makes a hiding place that only the Drome boys know about.

The day after Ben crawled away from the crashed car, the *Tarmouth Herald* announces three thousand pounds' worth of damage to the exterior cladding of the aquarium. Inside the Deepest Tank in Europe, lined with spray-on concrete, the fishes were barely shaken. Only the giant cod paused a little as the surface of their world was rocked by the impact of a Vauxhall Vectra on the pale Scandinavian pine outside.

Ben had turned to look for Luke after the impact and had found only an empty seat – maybe he'd been thrown clear and had got away already. With the wailing of sirens in his ears, Ben had crawled out of a window and had somehow reached The Crock. Hugging a gashed chin, he'd slipped indoors. Boyce had fixed him up and tipped him out on the moor road and told him to stay away. And under a cold moon, alone on airstrip 3, between the humps of silvered sheep, Ben Crocker had lifted the hatch in the turf and had slipped beneath the ground . . .

He'd snuffled on the damp bed in the bunker next morning until Joel Higginbottom had lifted the hatch. 'Crocker, you there? Did you ring me?'

'Whisky?' Ben looked at the bottle. 'What good is that, you dork?'

'Nicked it before I left the house.'

'I want food, don't I?'

'I'll have it,' Higginbottom said, unscrewing the bottle himself.

Ben had got rid of him at last and had rung Luke Couch at home. 'All right?'

'No thanks to you,' Luke had said. 'Nutted the dash, didn't I? You?'

'Chinned the wheel,' Ben said.

No one had said anything else for a minute and the lonely ring of the bunker had sounded down the line.

'I'm out at the Drome. Can you come over or what?'

Something in the way Ben's voice had broken briefly brings Luke out for the bus with a pasty and a doughnut in his pocket. The 312 to Moorland Cross jolts along past the golf course. Luke gets off at the roundabout.

The usual wind whips over the approach road to the Drome. As Luke nears a huddle of Nissen huts, the lonely concrete runway of airstrip 3 stretches away to his right.

Ben's expecting him. A hatch in the turf beside airstrip 3 opens as he approaches and a deep shaft yawns over a ladder plunging quickly away to a dim light at the bottom.

'Yo.' Luke puts on a smile under the large plaster covering his temple.

Ben turns wordlessly and leads the way down again. The ladder rings under Luke's feet. Fifteen metres underground a dank room opens off the bottom of it.

'Brought you a pasty.'

'Thanks.'

'Some place.'

Ben looks at him.

'Bonus,' says Luke, his voice sounding flat in the dull little room lit with a torch showing only a bed and a chair. 'Wyndham sent you an El Presidente.'

Ben sits on the bed and unwraps the hot dog. Around its wrapper curls a twenty-pound note.

'That's from Griff,' Luke adds.

'"From the Red Hats, Regards, Griffin Flashman",' Ben reads. 'Who's the Red Hats?'

'New posse.'

'Why would they help me?' Ben says, unwrapping his pasty as well.

'Hoping you'll help *them*,' Luke says. 'After you've been to the cops.'

'Not going to happen,' Ben says. 'I crossed the line this time.'

Luke watches Ben bolt his pasty. The gash in his chin's been dressed.

'Saw you get out of the car,' Luke says.

Ben nods with his mouth full.

'Went to The Crock, did you?'

Ben nods again. 'You?'

'Monster headache all night. Told the olds I walked into a lamppost.'

Around them the bunker walls sweat with moisture. Built to withstand a nuclear attack, the damp room with its bunk bed and single shabby chair hasn't been used since the sixties. Opposite Luke the door to the bottom of the ladder opens to the right into a 'toilet' containing a bucket. The hatch of turf above makes certain that no one who isn't in on its secret ever guesses or stumbles upon the whereabouts of the bunker beneath.

Dispensing with his El Presidente in three giant bites, Ben starts on his doughnut.

'You could 'fess up,' Luke says.

'They'll throw the book at me this time.'

'You might not get much.'

'I will.'

'They'll understand.'

'They won't.'

Luke imagines pleading for Ben in court, getting him off miraculously, the way courtroom dramas seem to work out when the cool young attorney unearths vital new evidence: *He comes from a disadvantaged family. He never had a mother or a father. He's not bad, he just panicked. He thought it was his fault his mate died. He didn't care after that . . .*

'You can't rescue me – Si tried that,' Ben says, bringing out a photo. 'Ever show you this?'

A teenage boy with sandy hair and a narrow face smiles out of the photo-booth snap.

'That was a couple of years ago,' Ben says, pocketing the photo next to his heart. 'His hair's — his hair *was* — a lot different, when —'

Luke stands up to go. 'Two o'clock shift this afternoon,' he lies.

'You still at Make It All?'

'Till September,' Luke says.

'September now,' Ben says. 'Come back tomorrow, will you?'

'You can't stay here.'

'Come back tomorrow,' Ben says again.

'See you, mate.'

'Tomorrow.'

Luke boards the 312 back to town with a spinning head and mixed feelings about leaving Ben. The Drome posse'll be out there this evening, joking and barfing and setting fire to the settee on the runway. That's something, at least.

Now for the latest at home. Luke gets a sinking feeling walking down the street. Soon as he puts his head round the front door Danny says, 'Guess what?'

'What?' Luke says, pulling up his plaster in the hall mirror and examining the impressive yellow and blue bruise underneath.

'This bloke called last night about Julian Coombes.'

'Julian who?'

'It's Windy,' Danny says excitedly. 'They're after him from the children's home – Barnard Walsh.'

'He came round before,' Luke says. 'When you lot were at the zoo.'

'That was cool,' Danny says. 'Did you know a zebra's head weighs twenty pounds?'

'What's happening about Wyndham?'

'Mum talked them into letting him stay.'

'What?'

'He's having another week – then he's going back. He was watching telly when the man came. He stood up and said that the animals in the zoo had more choice over their lives than he did.'

'And?'

'Then Dad came in. "Julian?" he said. "No trouble at all. Taken to him, haven't we, Danny?" "Auntie Marion said he'd love it here," Mum goes. "Sorry we forgot to fill in the forms" – holiday custard, is it?'

'Custody,' Luke says.

'Then Mum speaks to Auntie Marion, not Bonnie who'd rung up before – and Auntie Marion said it was her fault Julian'd come, and the Social Services guy said that as it was some kind of muddle over holidaying with relatives of Mrs Nettlefold's he'd make an exception in this case.'

'So what, they're letting him stay?'

'And he's got an allowance and everything and we're redecorating the spare room next, and Wyndham's having it as his bedroom whenever he comes to stay, and the *real*

Wyndham's coming over one day and we're all going out to the beach.' Danny draws breath at last. 'And we might visit him when he goes back, and he can come here for Christmas too.'

'So everything comes good for the gas-man.' Luke feels it all wash over him. Nothing seems very important compared with the thought of Ben sitting alone in his bunker. 'How come you like Wyndham, now?'

'Him and me hang out with Brad.'

'Brad?'

''f you were *ever* around, you'd know him – Nice bruise,' Danny says. 'What did you *do* last night?'

The compressed action of the previous day runs through Luke's mind like a film – 'fishing' with Ben on the Boxtrees Estate; Jasper Flashman locking up Make It All at six; Vollie kicking in the side of a car. Basketball, the Midtown Maulers scoring a three-pointer on the whistle, squealing wheels in the multi-storey car park afterwards, the moor, the railway tunnel – the Leyton Way back to town with a chopper overhead, shrieking brakes on Marrowbone Slip and the bleached pine boards of the aquarium wall welcoming the side of the car . . .

'You all right?' wonders Danny.

Slightly concussed, Luke thinks. 'I'm going upstairs to crash.' He turns on the bottom step. 'Carrie's coming for tea one day soon. What's the date today?'

'It says "Theory Test" today,' Danny shouts, checking the calendar in the kitchen. 'That current or what?'

'Omigod – what time?'

'Two o'clock at the driving centre. One forty-five now, you can make it if you –'

The front door slams.

'– try,' Danny finishes.

The screen winks back at Luke as the four-option question blinks stupidly from a list headed Page One of Four:

If a pedestrian crosses the street *but not at a crossing*, should you:

a) not stop
b) honk your horn
c) stop and shout at him
d) give way

Clicking d), Luke steals a glance across the room. One or two other people doing the stupid Theory Test as well as him, each with their head in a booth busy clicking dozy options on computer. Luke moves on to Question 14:

If parked *in fog* by the side of the road, which lights should you leave on to show that you are there?

a) disco lights
b) the Light of Asia Curry House
c) Pilsner-Lite
d) haven't the foggiest

Actually optioning 'hazard lights', Luke hurries to the end of the test before he falls down with boredom. Questions about stopping distances don't come up at all – a monkey with an itchy finger could pass this test.

Stepping outside, he finds Carrie. 'Did you just do that test?'

'Easy, wasn't it?' says Carrie, applying lip gloss. 'Just run off after basketball, why don't you?' She snaps away her lip gloss. 'Ben crashed a car, didn't he? I heard a big fuss in the night. This morning he's gone somewhere –'

'He's fine,' Luke says. 'So I heard.'

'So what, you saw the car chase and then you went home?'

'Remembered something,' Luke mumbles.

'I'm so tired of it all. I don't think anything'll change.' She falls into step beside him. 'I've got to get away from this White Hats thing.'

'I think that's a good idea,' Luke says cautiously.

'We could still see each other. It could be fun. You could come up and see me.'

'See you where?'

'I don't know – anywhere.'

She glances at him. Luke kisses her. They walk on after a moment.

'I can't come to yours any more.'

'No,' Carrie says.

'Vollie mad with me?'

'Wants to skin you alive. Luke?'

'Yeah?'

'It'll be all right, won't it?'

'Everything's cool,' Luke says. 'Promise.'

Turning into Home Sweet Home Terrace after leaving Carrie, Luke finds an R-reg red Peugeot 306 parked outside his house. Exhilarated at the sight of his half-a-car, he saunters up like an old friend and tries to be offish about it. So. We're gonna be spending some time together. Luke walks all round the car in one direction and all round it in the other. When he comes back to where he started, the 306 looks just as rude. Nice interior. Smart bodywork. Sunroof, car mats, radio/tape cassette-player. Forty-seven thou on the clock, hardly run-in, so let the games begin . . . Wonder what she'll do on a flat run down a broken concrete airstrip –

'Eighty, comfortably.'

Luke turns to find Danny coming out of the house with, behind him –

'Brad,' smiles Brad. 'Congratulations,' he adds. 'Plenty of poke for a first car. Your mum's got good taste.'

'How would you know?' Luke looks at him coldly.

'Brad came round with the cheque the other day,' Danny squeaks. 'He wanted to see the car –'

'I live just round the corner. I thought I might as well.'

'Brad, Brad, the insurance man,' Luke realizes, wondering where he's seen him before.

'He just beat me at Ghostrider level 6,' Danny babbles. 'No *way* can you strafe Headless Hector before the House of Horror, but then he *did* –'

'You just beat me at *Tryst*,' Brad says, pushing Danny.

'Mum know it's coming today?' Luke says, walking around his car.

'Fancy a spin?' Brad says.

Luke meets the challenge in Brad's eyes. 'Get my L plates,' he says to Danny.

The steering wheel feels cool in Luke's hands. Under his feet the pedals of his car feel responsive and easy to shift, anticipating his change down or up, the swing of the chassis round bends. Through his sunroof beams a friendly afternoon sun as Brad gives him directions: 'Stay in the outside lane. At Moorview roundabout we'll take the road to the old aerodrome. Slow down now, and indicate –'

Luke brakes in good time before the junction, takes the roundabout indicating correctly and pulls away smoothly afterwards, enjoying the power under his bonnet as he takes her up to top, and his thoughts coast away and next to him *Carrie leans across, turning up the volume, just the two of us she says, no one to stop us or tell us where to go, just the sea and the moor and freedom opening out forever, wherever we want to go* –

'Feel good?' Brad glances across at him.

'Creamy,' Luke acknowledges, coming back to earth and watching road signs. *Black circle with a line through it, end of city speed limit* – 'Danny, sit back, you moron. Are you belted up or what?'

Danny grudgingly does up his seat belt. 'Won't it go faster than this?'

'Not in a forty-mile-an-hour limit.'

'Hasn't got a CD player,' Danny grumbles. 'Drop me at Darren's house, will you?'

'Where is it?'

'The end one – Moorview Villas – here.'

'You're all right to pull over.' Brad checks behind as Luke indicates and pulls up smoothly in front of Darren's house.

'Nine or ten o'clock's good,' Danny says, climbing out. 'See you later, yeah?'

'Having a laugh, aren't you? Shut the door.'

'Mum collects me,' says Danny.

'Get the bus back,' says Luke. 'I'm not Mum, all right?' Taking advantage of a gap in the traffic, he pulls away, leaving Danny a little dazed.

Brad checks his nearside mirror. 'Door's opening – Darren's coming out – Danny's going inside.'

'Nice that you're looking out for my brother for me,' Luke says. 'Like I can't do that myself.'

Brad looks at him. 'Left on the Drome road now?'

'Or down this track,' Luke says, swinging on to a tyre-worn short cut and throwing Brad from side to side along the rutted paths of a forestry plantation.

The reservoir gleams through the pine trees. Brad's hands tighten on the side of his seat, a livid burn standing out on the back of his right wrist.

Emerging between black conifers on to the old railway track tapering into the mouth of the tunnel he sped through with Ben Crocker the day of the car chase, Luke drives as fast as he can towards it. Where the track disappears into the blackness of the tunnel, Luke handbrake-turns neatly between the overarching brick walls to face in the other direction.

'Where'd you learn that?' Brad says.

Luke turns to face him. 'I know who you are,' he says.

Brad's face changes. 'You do?'

'Wait here, all right?' Luke says coldly. 'There's someone I've got to see.'

12. Walk of Faith

To Ben in the Bunker
Can you come out now. Something to show you. Everything depends.
Luke.

After a stiff fifteen-minute walk to the Drome, Luke shoves
the note down the hatch. Then there's nothing to do but
wait. Hopefully Ben will have heard something and be on
his way up the ladder to investigate. Up to him if he opens
up. Right now Luke couldn't care. Sheep dot the runways
out towards the cheese factory and a few ponies block the
road. In a bunker under airstrip 3 there's a whole world of
blame and misery, but then again, so what? If Ben Crocker
could start again, he'd foul up some other way –

'Luke, that you?' Ben's face blooms like a mushroom out
of the darkness under the hatch.

'Can you come up?'

'Anyone here?'

'What do you think?'

Ben emerges slowly and looks around.

'What, you don't trust me?' Luke says.

157

Only the sound of sheep tearing the grass and a few rooks circling in the late-afternoon sunlight floats over the broken runways.

Ben notes the hardness in Luke's voice since the last time they met. 'What did you want to show me?'

'Come up,' Luke says again, dropping the hatch as Ben leaves it.

'Cold down there.' Ben looks at him. 'Torch batteries ran out and I'm saving the candle.'

'This way.' Luke turns to go.

'Higginbottom 'n' Dave'll be here soon –'

'It's me and you, all right?'

'Where are we going?' Ben says.

Luke walks fast with a cold knot of rage in his chest. 'I'm calling the shots now, not you.'

Ben overtakes him. 'What's up?'

Luke walks on coldly.

'I got you into shedloads of trouble, right?'

'Try almost killing me in a car chase,' Luke says, shouldering past. 'You took me robbing petrol, stooging around while you did stuff. You treated me like a mug from the off. I've *never* known *what's* going down –'

'What, and *now* you're angry?'

'I'm sick of people not being straight with me.'

'If you feel like you've got to help me, don't bother,' Ben says.

'Don't worry, I'm not. This is as far as I go. You can drive yourself to hell any way you want.'

'Nice,' Ben says.

'I'm in control when I'm driving,' Luke says. 'Ever since I met you my life came off at the bend —'

'I shouldn't've taken advantage,' Ben says. 'I knew you weren't Louis after you lied about breaking into the Albert —'

'I didn't break in.'

'You did.'

'All right,' Luke says, 'I did. But the fishing, helping you nick the Audi —'

'Luke Couch,' Ben jeers, 'country boy, moves in from the sticks, never does anything wrong.'

'Carrie thinks you tell her everything.'

'Leave Carrie out of this.'

They reach the barbed wire round the reservoir in silence, where Ben's jeans get snagged on the fence. Luke waits, feeling as if he'd like to run off and smash something.

Ben rips his jeans away from the fence and walks on. 'Anyway Boyce patched me up the other night. He says you're in with Griffin Flashman — then you bring me a bribe from the Red Hats — what am I supposed to think?'

'You don't know what you're talking about.' Luke's eyes pass over Ben as if he's part of the scenery. 'Path's over there.'

'Thing is —'

'It's a joke,' Luke says.

'What is? My life?'

Ben's face wants to understand. Something in his voice half-breaks. Something in Luke wants to be speeding along an open road with him with a fist through the sunroof and a finger up to life.

'The Red Hats,' Luke says. 'We only just started up.'

'I thought —'

'It doesn't matter now. Griff just tried to help you and you couldn't even see it. I just want this to be over now, all right?' Plunging into the conifer plantation, Luke heads down a gloomy path opening out ahead on to the old railway track.

'Where are we going?' Ben says again, joining him on the tracks where the tunnel looms ahead.

'Trust me, don't you?'

'Do I have a choice?'

'Least my family aren't a bunch of crims.'

'Take that back.'

'Come on, then,' Luke says, wanting to hit something badly. *Images of Ben saving his bacon when 'Louis' let slip he knew about the cars in the Albert. I told him first thing, Ben had lied.* 'What are you waiting for?'

'Don't be stupid. I could take you any time.'

Luke pushes him. 'See you try.'

Ben colours. 'Don't push it.'

Luke pushes him again.

'You don't mean that.'

Something about the way Ben doesn't resist stops Luke from wanting to push him again, or ever. 'Dunno what I'm going to do. I'm *so* going to blow everything.'

'What?' Ben says. 'You won't.'

'College — my driving test — Carrie —'

'You won't,' Ben says. 'It'll be all right.'

'I messed up before, at school –'

'Get away from here, it'll be fine. Forget you ever saw me.'

'That stuff about your family –'

'Forget it, it's true. Too late to change things now.'

'It's not too late,' Luke says.

'What d'you mean?'

'Come on. We're almost there.' Luke walks on towards the railway tunnel and stops within range of its odour of earth and coal. He looks back for Ben. 'Come on!'

Ben joins him reluctantly. 'I'm not walking through that tunnel.'

'We *drove* through it the other day.'

'That's different.'

'Why?'

'I – don't like the dark,' Ben says.

'There's only one bit in the middle where it's *completely* dark,' Luke says. 'It's a cycle path, no holes or anything. I did it on the way here. Takes about ten minutes.'

'How long's the dark bit?'

'Not long.'

'And there's something you want me to see on the other side?'

Luke looks at him. 'Are you going to bottle it or what?'

Ben steps into the shadow of the black mouth of the tunnel. A short distance ahead of him impenetrable blackness falls like a wall, extinguishing everything inside it.

'Keep going till you see the light,' Luke says. 'You can't see your feet or anything else, but I'll be right beside you.'

'Five minutes when you can't see a thing?'

'I'll help you,' Luke says. '*Trust me.*'

Ben looks at him. He turns and takes three steps, is swallowed into the darkness. The cool kiss of the air in the tunnel breathes over Luke as he follows.

In the blackness that instantly surrounds him, the sliver of light behind them makes for a comforting lifeline. With every step it gets thinner and the darkness ahead more solid. The light winks away at last with the slight curve in the track. *We're for it, now,* Luke thinks. *Yea though I walk in the shadow of the valley of the tunnel —*

'You there?' Ben's voice calls.

'Keep straight on – no problemo.'

Luke's voice sounds flat and weird. Deepest blackness surrounds him and presses itself into his eyes and his throat. The dank breath of the tunnel enters his bones. In the brick vault overhead their footfalls ring big like giants'. With each step into the blackness on trust, Luke imagines hidden holes, holes he might've missed on his way through earlier, when a cheery cyclist had passed and had shown him the whole of the tunnel by the light of a bicycle lamp.

'Still here,' he echoes.

'Much longer?' Ben says.

'Dunno.'

Time seems suspended, stepping along in the blackness with no sight or sense of his own body. And it seems to Luke that he doesn't exist, and at the same time he's falling into a church-big nothingness, and floating with nothingness around him – a disembodied brain moving through blackness, made of blackness, with nothing but blackness to see. Then he can't be sure if he's *moving or existing at all* –

'Ben! All right?'

'Here.'

Here, here, clamour the echoes trapped forever in the middle of the tunnel. One foot in front of another. Don't dare to talk at all. Sense the walls in the darkness. Trust you won't find a hole. Into the nothingness on faith alone –

'Luke?' *Luke, Luke* . . .

'What?'

'You don't have to help me – I'm going back.' *Help me, help me . . . back . . .*

'No – wait –'

'I can't do this –' *DO this, DO this . . .*

'You have to *jump* to save yourself –' The darkness rushes into Luke's mouth, but it seems like an inspiration. 'Like David Balfour – jump off the rock to save yourself. No going back, remember?'

It seems to Luke that they float on. A few metres more and the air freshens. Moments before the first wink of light, Luke smells the end of the tunnel.

'Ben, you there?'

In the greying light Ben smiles. Luke walks on towards a cold rush of air where a sliver of light widens like a theatre curtain opening on to a brilliant stage.

In the spotlight stands a figure. It turns and opens its arms. 'Ben! I'm sorry – I never meant –'

'Si.' Ben walks to meet him. 'Just don't say anything.'

13. The Drome Again

'I thought you were dead! I thought it was my fault!' Ben rages. 'How could you not *contact* me?'

'I thought about it plenty of times –'

'How could you let me go on thinking you'd died in the fire? Fun was it, living a secret life?'

'If you think I *enjoyed* seeing you around –'

'How could you let me *think* that? How could you stay away?'

'He thought they torched the casino because he owed them a Merc,' Luke explains.

'I didn't know what you were thinking,' Simon 'Brad' Bradshaw says, the dirty fringing around the standard lamp in the 'living room' on the airstrip lightly brushing the top of his sandy hair. Going over it for the fourth time, but as patiently as the first time Ben's accusations rolled over him, Si's eyes flicker sympathetically over Luke as well. 'It was a new start – the perfect opportunity. I couldn't turn down the chance to disappear. I didn't plan it – it happened. I was on the rota to work that night, but I'd called in sick with a stomach bug. When I heard about the fire, I didn't call in next morning.'

'I thought you were in the office!' Ben says. 'I *crawled through smoke* to find you! I almost didn't get out!'

'I thought you went home that night.'

'I ran through the cloakroom looking for you – smoke rolled in under the door –'

'I should've rung you.'

'You couldn't've rung me *after*?'

'I thought about getting a message to you. Then I remembered Vollie. He would've found out somehow.'

'Why disappear?' Luke says.

'My only chance to escape,' Si says softly. 'Vollie was pressuring me for a cut of the blackjack take. There's White Hats on the door of the Achilles Bar now –'

'Tell me about it,' Ben says.

'They never left me alone,' Si says. ''Specially because of *you*.'

'That'd be right,' Ben says bitterly.

'The fire seemed like a gift. It had nothing to do with you. That bloke from the Black Cat Casino who died in a fight on the steps after our bouncers threw him out? I knew there'd be trouble. Next thing, the Lucky Strike's torched. Doesn't take a genius to see the connection. When I realized I could keep my head down and "disappear", I went to Oxmouth and got a job.'

'Doing?'

'Insurance,' Si says. 'Then they post me here and guess what, I'm processing Luke's mother's claim for her stolen car. You've got a great family,' he says to Luke.

'I know.'

'They're worried about you,' Si says.

'Thought they were worried about Wyndham.'

'Julian's a survivor,' Si says. 'I was like Julian once.'

Sunset over Stowe Moor throws the long shadows of Nissen huts over the 'living room' on airstrip 1. Si takes burgers from a shopping bag and throws them on a grille over the burning 'coffee table'. Ben draws up his legs on the settee.

'Radical news about the smash at the aquarium,' Si says.

'That big?' Ben says miserably.

'All over town,' Si says. 'Lucky the tank didn't break. Could've had sharks and manta rays flopping about on the quay.'

'Doing them a favour,' says Luke. 'They just swim round and round.'

'You were there too?'

'Big time.'

'What'll we do?' Ben says.

'They haven't identified you yet. Keep shtum, they can't prove a thing. You don't have to say anything.'

'I want to,' Ben says. 'Then we can make a new start.'

Si turns the burgers and watches Ben through the flames.

'That burn on your hand,' Luke says. 'I thought it was from the fire.'

'From ironing a shirt,' Si says. 'Insurance is a dangerous business.'

'I'm serious about going to the police,' Ben says. 'I've used up all my luck. I could've killed someone —'

'I knew you'd do the right thing,' Si says. 'It's all still to play for, whenever you're ready: college, travel —'

'India?' Ben says.

Bunning a burger and handing it to Ben, 'India,' Si says, 'why not?'

'I used to nick alloys from car yards, me,' a stringy lad named Whiz lets on. 'Nicked a stack of 'em one night with Dave Merchant's van? Clangy old things. Terrible racket. Had a flat tyre on the way home and they all slide out of the back when I'm tryin' to find the spare. Hell to pick up quietly, them things. Crashin' around all over the road I was, till this bloke stops and gives me a hand. "Slippery beggars, in't they?" he goes. Turns out he's car yard's brother on his way home with the pickup. "Thanks," I'm going. I never let on. Fernly Wallace, that was. Worst over-charger in the business. Then I had a thing for laptops from Travelodge car parks —'

As the Drome boys share burgers round the fire later that night and the stars twinkle coldly behind the control tower on the horizon, the stories swapped in the firelight seem like tall tales from a Western.

'Me and Pete Screech raided a filling station,' Joel Higginbottom says softly. 'Jet station near home it was. Me and Pete were thirteen. Pete goes, "Put these tights over your head." Minute we go in with fake guns, Mr Gift recognizes us straight away. "Known you since you were

five, Joel," Giftie goes. "See through that stocking, no problem. You should've got Barely Black, not Nearly Natural."'

Everyone laughs.

'Dun't matter about the colour, it's how *tight* they are,'
Whiz objects.

'These were XL,' Joel says.

Everyone laughs again.

'Giftie never reported it. Haven't nicked anything since.'

'Not motors?' Ben says.

'Race my brother's old bangers, don't I?'

'Lucky for some,' Ben says.

Cattle low somewhere over the reservoir. Even the car
wrecks lining the distant barbed wire blend under the
moonlight into the dim and silvery 'furniture' surrounding
the living room on the airstrip. The glow of the fire seems
to lock them in a circle of friendship and cider, and the
two halves of Luke's life, Luke and Louis, come together
into something that finally makes sense as Si and Ben clink
bottles on the settee and raise them in a toast: 'To Luke!
Cheers, mate! It's all down to you!'

What is? Luke wonders happily.

The days whirl away after that, it seems to Luke, things
falling into place in the right order for once, like the suits
in a pack of cards – Danny going back to school with
not too much complaining and a cool pair of Kickers to
start Year Ten; packing it in at Make It All, Greavesie joking,
'See you at Christmas,' saying' 'No chance,' and not meaning it; registering for his course at college in a confusing

morning's whirlwind of queuing for bits of paper; the examiner on the day of his driving test, after thirty-five minutes' manoeuvring around town and the Blue Monkey Industrial Estate, pushing up his glasses and saying, 'I'm pleased to tell you, you've passed your driving test with three minor penalty points.'

Damn, Bowden passed with two. 'Top banana,' Luke had grinned, pocketing the keys to the Peugeot and freedom triumphantly on his return home.

Other events pack the days which fall one after another towards mid-September like smiling Jacks into a hat. The White Hats losing their hold over the Achilles Bar. Vollie's power on the streets broken with the loss of his business and an upcoming prosecution thanks to information supplied by his own brother, Ben, in a trade-off which lets magistrates take a kindly view of Ben's involvement in a car crash . . . Carrie coming to Wyndham's farewell tea with Ben, preparing him, Luke, for the time when she might go away, while Dad surreptitiously reads his paper as dessert arrives on the table.

'They pinned that car smash at the aquarium on some unnamed tearaway,' Dad says conversationally. 'Mitigating circumstances or something. Must be laughing his head off.'

Mum nudges him. 'Carrie – Phishfood or Cookie Dough ice cream?'

'What's the Phishfood got in it?'

'Nougat, lumps of chocolate –'

'Go for it,' Carrie says.

'Tearing around stealing cars,' Dad says. 'What kind of homes do they come from?'

'You'd be surprised,' Luke says, meeting his father's eyes coolly.

'There's all kinds of homes and all kinds of reasons and people,' Wyndham says feelingly. 'And some people don't even *have* any.'

'Fair comment, Julian,' Dad says.

'You always tell him he's right,' Danny complains.

'Julian's a guest.'

'No, he isn't. He's got his own room. You should tell him off.'

Dad puts down his spoon. 'Where should I start?'

'He's got my mattress,' says Danny. 'He went in my room and swapped them.'

'It fits my bed better,' says Julian.

'My bed, you mean.'

'Doesn't matter anyway, now I'm going.'

'When are you going?' says Danny.

'Monday morning,' says Julian Coombes. 'Have all your stuff back and play chess on your own – that soon enough for you?'

'Piece in the paper about these Red Hats,' Dad says, reading it under the table. 'Must be your lot, Julian. "New Volunteers Reclaim the Streets." Seems Griffin Flashman's got some weight with the council. All kinds of schemes in the air for a skateboarding area and a playground. Inspired by the Gashouse Lane Volunteers saving the streets during the war – *You* know about that, Luke.'

'Used to,' Luke says, absorbed in watching Carrie.

'Didn't know it was Monday,' says Danny. 'You can have the mattress till then.'

'*And* the PlayStation?'

'Don't push it.'

'Push *you*.'

'Shove it, Coombesie,' says Danny, throwing a leftover chip.

'Family mealtimes always like this?' Carrie jokes.

'Worse usually,' Julian grins, enjoying the luxury of belonging at least as much as Ben and Jerry's ice cream.

'Coming for you Monday at nine, are they?' Ben Crocker looks up.

'I can come back at Christmas,' says Julian. 'Or any time I want.'

'Last day tomorrow,' says Luke. 'Coming for a burn — I mean a nice, quiet trip in the country in my new car?'

'I want to see cows,' says Julian. 'And pigs and geese and sheep, and that crusty stuff in the supermarket —'

'Clotted cream?' says Mum.

'Where they make that, as well.'

'Carrie,' says Mum, 'how's the job?'

'Good, but it finishes next week. Then I'm going away.'

'Where to?'

'Oxmouth, to stay with a friend,' Carrie says evenly, looking at Luke. 'She's showing me round the university. I'm starting an Access course.'

'Sounds good, doesn't it, Luke?'

Luke looks at Carrie. *Liv, isn't it?* his eyes say. 'Back of the net,' he says. 'Now I can drive up to visit.'

'You'll miss home,' Ben says.

'No, I won't.' Carrie checks an earring nervously, the cuffs of her white shirt narrowly missing her ice cream. 'I won't miss anything around here except —' She takes Luke's hand under the table.

'That Merc — I never stole it,' Ben says.

'Ben,' Carrie says, 'this isn't the time —'

'I know you believed that story about me crashing it. You had it wrong all along. I ran off. I chucked the keys in the hedge. It's the only thing I've done that I'm proud of.'

'Not the *only* thing,' Carrie says, taking Ben's hand too.

'I know I'm in the dark,' Dad says brightly. 'Shall we take coffee in the living room?'

'Just a minute.' Luke's mother takes out a present and sets it in front of Julian. 'Something we thought you might like to take with you.'

Coombesie glows. 'For me?' Tearing off the wrapping, he exposes a familiar shape. He opens the case. '*Really?*'

'Really,' says Dad. 'Luke and I —'

'And Danny,' says Danny.

'— and Danny, we'd like you to look after it for us. Grandpa'd want you to have it to remind you that people have dads who leave them funny things.'

'No problem,' breathes Julian Coombes, turning in his hand the Turk's-head pipe of his dreams, bitter with the smells of the Orient, handed down from man to man.

'I can look after it for you. It's the best thing I ever had,' he says, replacing it reverently in its case.

'You're lucky it'll remind you of dads,' says Ben, and only the tick of the clock sounds behind a whole world of sadness in his voice. 'Know what the point of parents is? To be there. Day after day, *every* day. Just,' Ben says, 'to be *there*.'

In the garden at Home Sweet Home Terrace after tea, Carrie says, 'I brought you something.'

'What?' says Luke.

'My journal – I want you to have it. I want to be straight about *everything* now I'm going away. Sure you're OK with it?'

'Way to go,' Luke says. 'You're too smart to stick around here.'

'Start from here.' Carrie finds a page. 'You read the rest already.'

Luke takes the *Confessions*. 'History of us,' he says.

'My old life,' says Carrie. 'I'm leaving it behind. *You're* the only thing that's coming with me –'

'I'll be up every weekend. You won't be able to get rid.'

Carrie kisses him lingeringly. 'When d'you start college?'

'Monday week. Want a lift up to Oxmouth?'

'I was hoping you'd say that. Soon as I pass my test, I'll drive down to see *you*.'

'Any day now, I bet. Just don't touch the kerb when you reverse-park or they dock you a penalty point . . .'

Talking three-point turns and hill starts, making their

way through the gate and over the hill above sparkling Tarmouth Sound, Luke Couch and Carmen Crocker make plans while the sailing boats ply to and fro.

14. Joyride

First page of the New Confessions, excepting I'm calling them the New Leaf, turning over of. No more moaning about anything. Only positive things.

An amazing change in Ben. He's reading travel guides — India, Thailand, Indonesia. He's got some stuff to get through. But this time next year he'll be clear of it.

I'm glad I gave Luke my old diary. It wipes the slate clean somehow, plus now there's no secrets between us. Luke knows I'm straight with him, straight with myself, forever.

The road's opening in front of me now, a road to a life I can make for myself, somewhere I can make a home, friends, something that won't depend on anyone else but me. Luke'll always be in it. Some people are warm like fires. They make the centre of things and everyone comes back for more.

Luke's a part of my life now. I'm putting on the handbrake and parking with hazard lights on in HIS life, so that everyone knows I'm there.

— Confessions of Carmen Crocker

'So this is where I used to wash cars —' Luke says, touring his old village grandly, pointing things out from the car. 'Liv's old house, my house, youth club — had to be sad to go there —'

'How long did you live here?' says Julian Coombes, hanging on as Luke wheels sharp left around a corner made by a cottage.

'All my life up till now. Paxman's house, Mrs Oliff's house – Yo, Mrs Oliff, doing some gardening?'

A white-haired woman drops her trowel. 'Luke – you learned to drive! Good for you!'

'I just got my car. Goes a bit,' Luke says carelessly.

'Nice colour,' says Mrs Oliff. 'Red, with a green bonnet. I think it might catch on.'

'Being resprayed next week. Danny drove it into a wall.'

'How is Danny?'

'Working. He does the ice-cream van Sundays.'

'Showing your friend where you used to live?'

'This is Julian,' Luke says. 'He's never seen a cow.'

'Plenty of cows down the road,' says Mrs Oliff. 'Nice field of sheep round the corner.'

'We found one the wrong way up,' Julian volunteers. 'Luke climbed in the field and turned it over and probably saved its life.'

'Sheep can get stuck sometimes ... How's city life, Luke?'

'All right, but I miss my mates.'

'That'll come, in time.'

'If they can stand the smell,' Julian adds.

'Get out and walk. Showing him stuff, now I can drive,' Luke explains.

'You won't want a lift to town to get your stickers, then,' Mrs Oliff says.

Luke grins, remembering turning up on her doorstep when he was eight. 'Big enough and ugly enough to get my own.'

'You heard it here first,' says Julian.

Luke dips the accelerator. 'See you, Mrs Oliff.'

Mrs Oliff watches as he speeds off down the lane. 'Good luck, Luke,' she says.

Throttling out round Cap Hill and on to ancient Viper Down beyond, Luke takes the north coast road, changing easily up through the gears.

'Went to school over that hill. Did an extra year. Too much yakking and boozing.'

Julian Coombes looks at him. 'Chance'd be a fine thing at the Walsh. Where are we going now?'

'Surfing at Langlaze Sands.'

'But –'

'We c'n hire surfboards when we get there. Wanted to go the beach, didn't you?'

Checking his mirrors, Luke overtakes a lorry. Opening out on to the Atlantic Highway, he turns the music all the way up. The sea sparkles beyond Tarmouth, where once a speedboat named *Biscuit* cut the waves . . .

'It was down to you,' Luke shouts, over the mix.

'What was?'

'The New Volunteers. Wyndham Nettlefold – hero under an assumed name.'

'A what name?'

'A disguise. Like "Airman Shaw" for Lawrence of Arabia. You got the Red Hats up and running.'

'Griff did, you mean.'

'You started Griff.'

'I did, didn't I?' muses Wyndham of Arabia. 'He didn't take much starting.'

Fending off questions about possible Arabian headgear, taking the long road out to the sea in a joyful fifth gear, in control and steering into his future, Luke feels *more like himself* than at any other time in his life. The wind tears in through the sunroof and the music thuds warm through his seat and the sun strikes the road ahead in one perfect moment of freedom and speed *beyond anything with the power to stop him.*

Luke glances sideways. Julian feels it too. 'Fist through the sunroof! On the count of three! One – two –'

'*Three!*'

Two fists punch through the sunroof as the car speeds down to the sea.

CARWASH
Lesley Howarth

Summer, and time for Luke to start up his carwash
business again. Time for some serious money-making.
But this year, Cool Hand Luke, best car washer in
the west, finds that the carwash sets off changes he
never expected.

Luke is used to being in control. He knows who's cool
and who isn't. He enjoys winding people up, but can he
handle it when people start winding *him* up? What's
he going to do when he discovers a new side of himself –
as revealed by clever, cool, unattainable Liv?

Choosing a brilliant book
can be a tricky business...
but not any more

www.puffin.co.uk

The best selection of books at your fingertips

So get clicking!

Searching the site is easy – you'll find
what you're looking for at the click of a mouse,
from great authors to brilliant books and more!